NEUROSIS

SEEING ISN'T ALWAYS BELIEVING.

AMY HALE

HaleFire
PUBLISHING

Neurosis
Amy Hale

Cover Designer: Regina Wamba

Editor: Cheree Castellanos, For Love of Books Editing4

Interior Design: HaleFire Publishing

Print ISBN: 978-1-952498-08-4

PREFACE

A NOTE TO READERS:

What you are about to read may contain sensitive subject matter that some may find triggering. This book deals with mental health issues, and has mentions of abuse, trauma, and self-harm/suicide. Please proceed with caution if these might be topics that would cause you discomfort.

As someone who deals with mental illness daily, I'd like to remind you that everyone is different in their health journeys. I've done my best to reflect that in this story. I've also worked hard to avoid adding further stigma to any mental health issue while still remaining true to the story.

Enjoy this thrilling adventure.

Sincerely,
    Amy Hale

MACY

"Thanks for seeing me on such short notice." Macy McCall sat on the edge of the beige tufted chair in her psychologist's office. Anxiety riddled her already tense body. Her hands moved of their own volition, the hem of her cotton shirt bearing the brunt of her fidgeting.

"I was fortunate to have an opening. How have you been since our last visit, Macy?" Dr. Daniel Yates raised his eyes to hers.

"Struggling." Her answer came out as a whisper.

"Tell me about it." He smiled, but his voice had an edge of authority.

Macy clasped her hands together, squeezing her fingers to stop their shaking.

"What made you feel an extra appointment was necessary this week?" He leaned forward, his tone softening. "Remember, I'm here to help you figure it out."

She nodded and willed the lump in her throat to disappear. "I saw her again." She kept her tone soft, as if her fears would manifest before her eyes at the mere mention of them.

"Her? You mean the woman that looks just like you?" He leaned back against his chair.

"Yes. My double." She shook her head and pressed her lips together in a tight line. "Seeing her. It just... scares the hell out of me."

"Remember what we discussed last time? It could possibly be a person who resembles you. We all have at least one doppelgänger, so to speak."

"I know, but..." her bottom lip trembled, and she instinctively placed her index finger to her lips, chewing on what she had left of a ragged fingernail.

"But..." He smiled and was patient as she took a moment before she continued.

She dropped her hand to her lap. "Something feels off. When I see her, my anxiety spikes and I shake like a child who thinks there's a monster in her closet. It feels like I'm witnessing something I shouldn't. Something sinister." She paused and looked down at her hands, which were once more mangling the hem of her shirt. "I've never considered myself a superstitious person, but aren't doppelgängers supposed to be bad luck or something? Like an omen?"

He grinned. "Do you believe in luck? I personally think luck doesn't exist."

She shrugged. "I used to believe that, but in the last several years I've begun to wonder. I mean, I seem to be plagued by bad luck. Or maybe I'm fucking cursed."

"You don't really believe that, do you?" He studied her face.

A deep, dissatisfied sigh escaped her lips. "I guess not." She paused and let herself think a moment. "Maybe my meds aren't working as well as they used to? I could be hallucinating her, right?"

He nodded. "It's rare in patients with PTSD, but not impossible."

"So, if it's not real, how do I deal with this?" Her hands shook slightly as she brushed a stray hair from her face.

"You could use grounding techniques. It's important in this case that we first establish reality from fiction. If you see your doppelgänger again, work down a checklist. Can anyone else see her or hear her? Is she talking to you or about you? Do you feel you are in any danger?"

"Okay. I can do that." Macy cleared her throat. "I've felt like I'm in danger somehow, but I can't tell you why. I don't know if it's real or my anxiety."

He tapped his pen on his knee. "Try to remember that no matter what, you are in control of the situation. If it is an actual person, you can walk away or get help if that person makes you feel unsafe. If your checklist determines it's a hallucination, you can remind yourself that we are working to manage your condition, and you are in no real danger. You are not alone in this. Sound good?"

Macy nodded and swallowed hard. "Yes. I'll try."

"Good. Now tell me about this experience. How did this sighting differ from the first time?"

She sat back and blew out an unsteady breath. "Well, you know... the first time was brief. I looked up and saw her staring at me, then when I looked away for a moment she was gone. I thought for sure I was sleep deprived or there was some other rational explanation for seeing someone that was a carbon copy of myself. It was right down to my clothes and hairstyle. But this time I was in the library."

"So, you went to the library this week, as we discussed?" She noticed the pride he took in her taking such a big step. His smile radiated approval for her bravery.

"I did. As you suggested, I spent some time at the library

last night. It was working." A humorless chuckle conveyed her frustration. "I was enjoying a quiet environment that wasn't overwhelming but also contained a few people. There wasn't enough activity to create a sensory overload. Not enough people to make me feel threatened or overly anxious. At least, that's what I thought."

She took a moment to catch her breath. Just thinking about the night before was causing her chest to constrict. "I was there for almost two hours. I was reading and enjoying feeling somewhat normal for a change." A tear trailed down her cheek, that loss of momentary normalcy creating a grief she'd not expected to feel. "I'd just put down my book and had considered finding another before heading home when I saw her. She was sitting across from me, two tables away. She was just… staring at me."

"Did she make any acknowledgement or gesture toward you?" His brows furrowed as he leaned his forearms on his knees.

"No. She only stared at me. Or through me. I felt like she was judging me somehow and I didn't measure up." She closed her eyes for a moment, sure exhaustion and recent events were getting to her.

"What gave you the impression she was judging you? And why would you fall short?" He looked into her eyes.

"I don't know. It was just something in her gaze. In her posture. It seemed haunted and hollow and… angry." Macy rubbed her hands over her face and a small sob escaped. "Shit, as for why I'd fail an inspection, I'm sure there's no shortage of reasons."

Daniel nodded. "You're projecting your guilt again."

Macy used the palm of her hands to scrub away the tears now streaming down her face. "You think so?"

"You're possibly seeing yourself. A version that maybe

hates you for your past. Being the only survivor of a tragedy is a tough thing to come to grips with. That guilt can manifest in several ways." She thought she heard sympathy in his voice.

He looked her in the eye again. "Especially with loss such as yours."

Macy nodded and tried to focus on the air that struggled to enter and exit her lungs. "I guess that makes sense."

"I'm not with you when it happens, so I can only take a professional guess at what you're dealing with. But try to remember that your past does not define who you are. You couldn't control the events of that evening any more than you can control the weather."

Macy sighed loudly and gulped a greedy helping of air before she repeated the affirmations that had helped her when she consciously felt guilt over the loss of those she loved. "I know. I didn't start the fire. I didn't allow people to die. I did everything I could. I was only twelve."

"Exactly." He placed his palms together as if in prayer and touched his fingertips to his chin as he appeared to gather his thoughts. "If you feel up to confronting your other self, should it be a hallucination, remind that other self that you are innocent of all charges she places against you. Then repeat your affirmations to her."

"Okay. I will." Her voice was soft and didn't hold the determined conviction she knew he liked to hear near the end of a session, but she couldn't fake it. And the short time allotted to her in this impromptu appointment was nearing an end.

"Try to believe in yourself, Macy." He admonished. He looked at his watch. "Now, you still have the emergency number should you need it?" He stood.

"Yes, it's in my phone." She stood as well. Her stance

proved she was slightly unsteady on her feet, but she recovered quickly.

"Great. Call it should you need anything at all and we will make sure you are safe."

Macy did her best to give him a genuine smile. "Thank you again, Dr. Yates. I feel a bit better now. Still scared, but better. I have a plan at least."

He placed a hand to his heart. "I'm happy to help, Macy. Take care and I'll see you in a few days at our normal appointment."

"Yes." She picked up her purse and clumsily slung it over her shoulder. "See you Monday."

Dr. Yates opened the office door for her, and she slipped through without another word. It clicked softly behind her and she stood there silently, pushing all the fear as far from her mind as she could. "I'm in control" she told herself as she made her way down the hall and to the elevator. Her fingers clumsily pushed the button to call it to her floor.

She hated elevators. Macy always feared she'd get trapped in one. And if there was a fire while trapped? She didn't allow her mind to wander any farther in that direction. She reached her right hand up and touched the fabric covering her stomach. Her mind traced the raised skin that marred her porcelain complexion. The scars stretched from her bellybutton to her ribs on the right, one of constant reminders of the flames that seared her skin during the worst night of her life.

Sometimes she didn't think about her scars. But other times, like now, she couldn't help but feel them. It was almost as if her flesh was burning all over again. She never understood how a scar that was twelve years old could still cause her twinges of pain. But to be honest, there were a lot of things she didn't understand.

Her post traumatic stress disorder and anxiety began shortly after she lost everything. At the time her uncle had thought that she'd just needed time to heal, but after several months he'd realized she needed professional help. Witnessing almost everyone she loved die in an inferno that she barely escaped herself had knocked down the dominos of everything she'd thought she'd known. It created an unsafe, terrified reality within her mind.

Depression, paranoia, anxiety, and insomnia were constant, albeit unstable companions until she found Dr. Yates. His methods weren't drastically different from those of her past doctors, but there was something special about the way he worked with her. Or maybe she was finally ready to begin healing. Either way, he was compassionate and remarkably good at his job, and she knew she was fortunate to be in his care.

She stepped inside and pushed the button for the lobby. The elevator doors closed, and she held her breath, waiting for it to descend to the bottom floor. Once movement began, she tensed up, expecting a catastrophe that would not occur. It never did. The elevator never got stuck. It never fell or dropped suddenly. The doors never closed without opening again moments later at the floor she'd chosen. And yet, there she was, sick to her stomach for the few minutes she felt trapped within that small, confining space. She expected the worst, but also understood that her fears were mostly unfounded. Elevators rarely failed.

She glanced at the mirrored wall to one side of her and caught her reflection. Disheveled hair framed her pale face, and she had dark circles forming under her eyes. Her mind wandered to the doppelgänger she'd been seeing. Were hallucinations also now part of her PTSD package? That wasn't a usual symptom. She didn't know if she wanted them to be real or not. Both options were frightening.

Everything scared her; people, small spaces, sizeable crowds, loud noises, candles, flames… her list felt as if it went on forever. So many things seemed to trigger her, and she hated that her life mostly consisted of fear and medications.

The doors opened to the lobby, and she tried to smooth her long brown tresses as she stepped onto the shiny marble floors that lead to the exit.

Leaving was always hard for her. She felt safe in Dr. Yates' office, and there were very few places that fit into that category. Once she was outside the building it was important that she focus on the next step… getting on the bus.

Macy exited the building with a mix of lingering fear and renewed sense of hope. It was odd to be terrified and excited at the same time. Dr. Yates not only made her feel relaxed in his presence, but he gave her the impression that he genuinely cared. Her last psychologist had always made her feel like a test subject. His retirement was a blessing in disguise. She'd been comfortable with him, but she'd been seeing him for years with no noticeable progress.

She wrapped her coat around her body and gripped it tightly as she stepped out into the brisk Chicago air. This was the part of her outdoor ventures where she usually kept her head down enough to avoid eye contact but still prevent running into anything. She glanced up and once more caught her reflection in a storefront window. For a moment she had to look closely, afraid she was seeing someone other than herself. Her double. But it was indeed her; mousy, dull Macy McCall.

She'd never liked the way she looked. Her brown hair was straight and unexceptional, as were her dark eyes.

Macy's face was round, but not overly chubby. Her button nose sat centered above pale pink lips. She supposed a little make-up and some time in the sun would be beneficial, but she had yet to attempt either in quite some time.

Beneath her over-sized coat stood a small frame comprising full curves, average breasts, and what she thought were short, stumpy legs. Her uncle Robbie had tried repeatedly to take her shopping for a new wardrobe. "You might feel better if you wore some clothes that inspired confidence in yourself." He'd say.

Macy scoffed at the remembrance of their last conversation. He was a wonderful uncle, but he truly didn't understand how difficult it was just to leave the house some days. Going shopping was all but impossible at this point. Someday she would go out and enjoy all the things girls her age should take part in; clothes shopping, drinks with friends, girl's nights out that didn't end up with her running home like a coward. She was making progress, but those things would take time. She had too many fears to overcome. Triggers still seemed to lurk around every corner.

She focused her attention on getting home. The bus stop was only another block, and with any luck, she'd arrive with only a little time to spare. Riding the bus was another thing that triggered her anxiety, but it was her only option to get to her home from her doctor's office efficiently. She hated waiting at the stop with other passengers. Invariably someone always tried to strike up a conversation with her. When her replies were short and curt because of her anxiety, they'd accuse her of being antisocial, or as one man put it, "a stuck-up bitch." If they'd only known what she would give up to be an outgoing social butterfly. She'd found it's just easier to avoid people all together, whenever possible.

Her thoughts continued to wander as she carefully made

her way through the busy pedestrians around her. Today she seemed to take extra notice of young couples, especially those with children. Like most people, she wanted the American dream; husband, kids, a house full of family and friends. Unlike most people, she worried she was too unstable to take the necessary steps to make that happen. It left a gaping hole in her existence. Most days she could ignore the fear that she'd end up alone and just focus on surviving, but sometimes, like today, the solitude of her situation was overwhelming. Macy had a great boyfriend, but she wasn't sure that they'd ever advance past the casual dating stage. She had too many issues, and she worried Troy would eventually tire of her.

A child's laughter broke through her thoughts and she glanced up to see a toddler bouncing around his mother as they waited for the bus. His auburn curls danced around his cherubic face as he babbled and leapt around his mother's feet. Her attention was otherwise engaged in something on her cell phone, and the little tyke was having a hard time being patient.

"Ma ma ma ma ma" he sang loudly as he jumped and tugged on her coat.

"In a minute, baby," she said as she continued to gaze at the screen in front of her.

He stomped his tiny foot in frustration, then let go of her coat and hopped in haphazard circles, almost losing his balance several times. He stopped in front of Macy and looked up at her with a smile. Her heart melted a little. She wanted a family so badly, but the part of her that remembered all she'd lost chastised her every time she considered it.

His little arm raised up above his head and he opened and closed his fist in a sloppy wave hello. Macy gave a small wave back, hoping the surrounding adults wouldn't notice her. He smiled wider, squatted down as far as he could go without falling over, then jumped as high as he could, which in reality wasn't but an inch or so off of the concrete. He landed and for a split-second Macy thought he'd planted his feet firmly, then she saw him teeter on his tiptoes and lunge forward off of the nearby curb.

Shit!

Macy instinctively reached out to grab him and snatched him back just as the bus was pulling up to the stop.

Her heart raced as she pulled the little tot close and assured herself he was okay. He struggled within her grasp and she released him, although not ready to let him get out of arm's reach just yet.

An older woman bent down and whispered in Macy's ear. "Thank God for your quick reflexes! That little guy would be roadkill right now. It's a shame parents don't watch their little ones the way they should anymore. I blame all those damn smart phones and tablets, turns your brains to mush!"

Macy froze as the woman spoke. Her first instinct was to flinch and pull away quickly, but she was afraid of knocking over the little boy still standing close to her.

"Alan! Alan, what are you doing?" The young mother's voice was shrill now, and it made Macy cringe.

"Ma, ma, ma!" said the little boy as he resumed his bouncing.

The woman reached over and took her son's hand. "What are you doing bothering the nice lady?" She looked up from her son to Macy. "I'm so sorry. I hope he wasn't bugging you."

Macy shook her head.

The older woman glared at the young mother. "You should keep a better eye on him! He was almost run over by the bus, but this little gal snatched him out of the way just in time!"

Macy's eyes widened. *Oh, no. No. No. Please don't say anything. Just let them get on the bus.*

"What?" Alan's mother frowned at the old woman, then at Macy.

Macy attempted a smile. "He lost his balance is all. I caught him. No big deal."

"No big deal?" exclaimed the older woman.

The bus doors opened and Macy rudely pushed past them all to get inside. She focused her breathing and lightly hummed her favorite tune to block out the noises around her. As the other people loaded onto the bus behind her, she could hear the older woman berating Alan's mother. She took her seat in the back and glanced up to see Alan clinging to his mama and the young mother rolling her eyes at the old woman.

Macy inserted her earbuds, turned on her music, pulled the hood of her coat over her head, and leaned back into the seat. With closed eyes, she tried to shut out the world and focus on breathing and calming her rolling stomach. Her stop couldn't come soon enough.

2

DANIEL

*D*aniel locked his filing cabinet and tucked the keys into his pocket. It'd been a long day, and it felt as if exhaustion seeped into his bones. He enjoyed helping his patients, but there were some that taxed him emotionally. He couldn't stop thinking about his patient, Macy McCall. She appeared to be a lovely young woman who'd been handed a dirty deal early in life. Her quiet demeanor and kind face didn't belay the horrors she faced inside her head. It completely turned her life upside down at age twelve, and it was no wonder she'd needed help since.

From the beginning, he knew her recovery would take time. She'd seen so much loss, and her life had been hell because of it.

Daniel shuddered at the thought. His calling was to help people, but sometimes it was difficult being inside the heads of people with so much trauma, fear, and misery. He'd be lying if he said he didn't occasionally have nightmares about some of the things he'd heard from his patients. Compounded with his own bad dreams, he often needed an escape. Or at least a way to quiet those demons a little. That was usually in the form of alcohol, although he was careful not to overindulge most of the time.

He rattled the knob of the outer door to his office. Satisfied it was secure, he quietly walked down the hall. The tip of his cane echoed down the empty corridor as he moved. His cell phone rang just as he stepped through the sliding door of the elevator.

"Dr. Yates speaking."

"Hey Daniel, are you still meeting me at the bar?" asked a jovial male voice.

"Oh, hey Roger." Daniel glanced at his watch. "I don't know. It's getting late, and it's been one hell of a day."

"Danny boy, you need to blow off steam. Breathing in all that crazy for the entire day isn't good for you. You need to trade that in for some stale bar air and cheap perfume."

Daniel sighed. "Roger, you know how I feel about that term. Besides, you just want a wing man so you can get laid."

"Well, yeah, but no reason you can't get laid too. Listen, I promise to stop using the word crazy if you'll hang out with me for a while tonight." When Daniel didn't reply, Roger groaned. "C'mon man. I need my wingman! I need you to lure them in so I can-"

Daniel cut him off. "Good God, stop already. I'll be there. Give me fifteen minutes."

"Great. I'll pay for the beers, you show up looking like Adonis. Between the two of us we should end tonight on a high note." Roger hung up before Daniel could say another word.

He pressed the button that took the elevator to the lobby and leaned back against the rail that stood between him and the wall. With his cane securely hooked on the rail, he pressed his fingers to his temples and rotated them in a circular motion. With closed eyes he imagined the hot shower and bottle of whiskey waiting for him at his apartment. He really didn't feel like going out tonight, but hanging out with his best friend was usually good for a laugh, even if Roger was a bit of a douche bag at times. Grabbing a beer and people watching might be just what he needed. Maybe.

The ping of the elevator notified him he'd reached his floor. He opened his eyes and pushed off the back wall, placing his cane back onto the floor. He squinted as he stepped out and into the bright lights of the building that housed his office. One of the night guards sat at his station and Daniel always made it a habit to say hello to him.

"Nice to see you, Hank! How are the kids?" asked Daniel as he slowed his pace.

"Doing much better, Dr. Yates. The flu seems to have finally left our house. Thank you for asking." Hank smiled as Daniel neared his desk.

"Glad to hear it. Have a good evening." Daniel waved as he passed through the doors.

Glancing at his watch again, he debated on whether he should go home and at the least take the shower he desired before meeting Roger, or if he'd be better off going straight to the bar. He opted for going to the bar now, knowing full well if he stepped foot in his apartment, he might break his promise to Roger and go to bed for the evening.

Daniel flagged down a cab and waited for it to come to a complete stop before settling inside.

"Take me to The Green Door Tavern, please."

The cabbie nodded his head and pushed the button to start the meter. Daniel leaned his head back and closed his eyes as he felt the cab pull away from the curb. He really hoped tonight would be fun and take his mind off things for a while. If it didn't, he would have to be careful about promising an outing with Roger again anytime soon.

*P*eople packed the bar. The noise was obnoxious, and the evening was not as entertaining as Daniel had hoped. His heart just wasn't in it tonight. Every girl he looked at reminded him of poor Macy. Her hollow smile, void of any genuine joy, replaced every flirtatious smile shot his way. He wasn't sure why her case had stuck with him so much. Maybe because of her tragic loss, and she reminded him a little of Vanessa.

He rubbed his hand over his face, taking note that he needed to shave. *Vanessa would have hated this stubble*, he thought to himself. He chastised himself for even thinking her name. He no longer wanted her to control his thoughts. As much as he missed her, she had no right to any real estate in his mind.

Fingers trailed along his back, from his right shoulder to his left. He looked up to see a lovely woman with stunning blue eyes smiling at him.

"Hey there. You drinking alone?" She brushed a blonde curl back to reveal a bare shoulder peeking through her shirt, then leaned against the bar as she spoke.

"I'm with a buddy of mine." He tilted his head toward Roger, who was currently trying to catch the attention of a woman at the other end of the bar.

"He looks like a fun date. You been together long?" She took a small sip of her beer.

Daniel laughed. "Nah, he's not my type. He's too hairy."

Her brows raised in interest. "Is that so? There's always waxing."

He shook his head. "There isn't enough wax in the world."

She threw her head back and laughed. "Sounds like you

need a good woman instead."

Daniel shrugged. "That does seem to be my preference."

"I might know one, if you're interested. She's not too hard on the eyes, if I say so myself, and she has a great sense of humor."

He briefly closed his eyes. She was tempting. Very tempting. But he didn't do one-night-stands. "She sounds like a catch, but I'm not looking for something like that at the moment."

"How about a friendship? She appreciates a man who can make her laugh, and she doesn't have too many friends in the area right now."

He took another swig of his beer. "I'm good with friendship."

She stuck out her hand. "Hi, I'm Sarah. It's nice to meet you."

"Daniel." He shook her hand and found he liked how it felt against his. "It's nice to meet you too."

"Do you and your friend hang out here a lot?" Sarah took another sip.

"Sometimes. He's here more than I am." Daniel shifted his gaze to Roger, still working his game along the other end of the bar.

"This is my first time. In fact, this is my first night out since I moved here a couple of weeks ago." She smiled, but he could see doubt creeping into her features.

"Ah, a transplant. Welcome to the Windy City. Where did you call home before this?" He turned to see her better.

"Oh, here and there."

Daniel smirked. "Well, that's nice and vague."

"I've only just met you. I don't even know your last name. Under the circumstances, what would you tell me about your past?"

He raised his glass to her. "Point taken." He finished the contents of his drink. "My last name is Yates, by the way."

She raised her drink in kind. "Hello, Daniel Yates."

He raised his eyes to the mirror in front of him and saw a bright flash of red hair pass somewhere behind him. His stomach churned.

He shoved his empty glass toward the bartender. "I'm done for the night."

Roger put a hand on his back. "Introduce me to your lovely friend?"

Daniel pushed Roger's hand away. "Roger, this is Sarah. Sarah, this is Roger."

She gave Roger a small wave.

His smile widened. "Has this guy bought you a drink yet?" He placed his hand on Roger's shoulder once again.

"I have one." She smiled, but kept her eyes on Daniel.

"Has this idiot asked for your phone number yet?" Roger gave Daniel's shoulder a small shove.

"Okay, Roger. Cool it." Daniel grumbled.

"He hasn't. But I planned on giving it to him, anyway." She grinned as she handed Daniel a business card.

Daniel nodded in thanks as he placed her card in his pocket without looking at it. "Listen, I appreciate the company, but I've gotta run."

"Did I say something to run you off?" Asked Sarah.

"No, it's not you. Just not feeling great right now."

Roger frowned. "Really? You're bailing on me now?"

"Sorry," Daniel said. "It's a bad night for me."

Roger frowned. "Is your leg bothering you again?"

"Among other things." He replied.

Sarah's eyes glanced down and he could tell the moment she noticed his cane.

Roger nodded. "I've got your back. If you need me, call.

I'll be at your apartment in no time."

Daniel placed his money on the bar and pushed it toward the bartender. "I know. I appreciate it."

Roger turned Daniel to face him and handed back his money. "I told you I was paying for the drinks. And I mean it, man. No matter what." His gaze seemed to bore into Daniels as if willing him to understand and acknowledge. Daniel found it creepy.

"I promise. But I should be fine." He pushed Roger back and motioned to the brunette making eyes at them from a nearby table. "Go jump on that opportunity before she finds someone more interesting… or comes to her senses."

Roger straightened his shoulders and smiled as he walked toward the beauty beaming back at him, then said, "Well hello, young lady. Are you sure you're old enough to be in here?"

Daniel rolled his eyes as he turned to face Sarah. "It was nice to meet you, Sarah. Maybe I'll see you around again soon."

She nodded. "Maybe."

He navigated out of the hot, overcrowded room. The cool night air greeted him and he took a deep breath, clutching the head of his cane so tightly that his knuckles turned white. He exhaled and then inhaled again, trying to clear his lungs and his mind. Tonight was going to be a long one. He could feel it coming. He needed to get home soon.

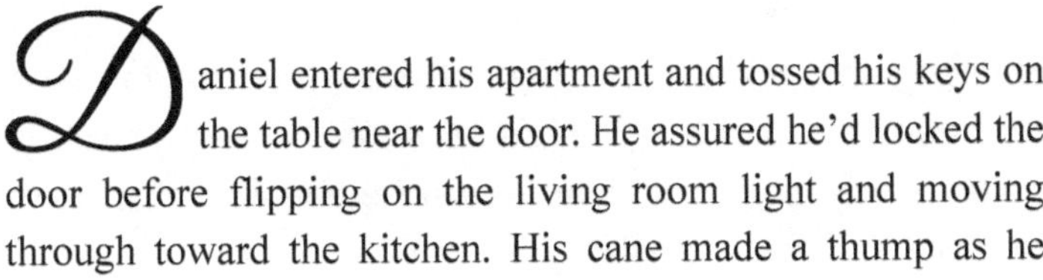

*D*aniel entered his apartment and tossed his keys on the table near the door. He assured he'd locked the door before flipping on the living room light and moving through toward the kitchen. His cane made a thump as he leaned it against the counter and pulled a small tumbler from a cabinet. He reached across the counter for a small decanter and poured a couple of fingers of the amber liquid.

The contents swirled in the glass as he examined it in the light. "God, Vanessa. Why?" He muttered. It was a question that repeated in his head daily.

He shook his head as he continued to study the whiskey in his hand. "I know you'd hate that I'm drinking, but… Fuck it. You left me. You don't get a say in what I do anymore."

He tossed back the contents and smiled as the warm liquid slid down his throat.

His fingers tightened over the cool, smooth glass just before he contemplated launching it across the room. Instead, he sat in on the counter, knowing the satisfying sound of glass shattering would only last a moment before he'd want to destroy something else.

"Damn you, Vanessa! Damn you for leaving and damn you for doing this to me!" He growled.

He gripped the countertop, pushing down the emotional pain that threatened to bring him to his knees. His right leg throbbed, and he closed his eyes to the images replaying in his mind. The road. Excessive speed. A large tree. Her thick, red hair splayed across the dash. Glass. Smoke. And blood. God, so much blood.

He grabbed his cane and clenched his teeth as he hobbled from the kitchen to his bedroom. Everything else could wait until tomorrow. He needed to sleep.

A chuckle escaped his lips as his eyes landed on the bed. The large, empty bed that taunted him on the best of nights. But tonight would be worse. Even sleeping pills couldn't save him from the darkness tonight. He knew the nightmares would surely come for him. When he felt like this, they always did.

3

MACY

Macy sat at a small table in a little Italian cafe close to her boyfriend's apartment. So far, she'd done a superb job of appearing calm, but inside her nerves were screaming at her to cut and run. It'd been over a week since she'd seen Troy. Their last date ended in an argument, and while he wasn't being distant, she admittedly was. She wasn't sure how to keep him happy and still do what she needed for her own mental health.

The cloth napkin Macy was twisting under the table was the only thing keeping her from fidgeting with the silverware and making a commotion. *He's late. Maybe he decided not to come.* Macy didn't know if that thought disappointed her or relieved her. She peeked at her watch and glanced at the restaurant door just as he entered the building.

He was so handsome. His shortly trimmed, sandy colored hair was perfect, not a strand out of place. She adored his sky-blue eyes. He had an angular, rugged face with just a smidgen of five o'clock shadow. He wasn't so tall that he was intimidating, but he still had a few inches over her five-foot-five frame. When he entered a room, all heads turned. Today was no different. They were all enjoying the view that was Troy Stevens. And she did not know why he was with her when she was certain he could always have his pick of any woman in the room.

He scanned the restaurant, and his eyes fell on Macy. He smiled widely as he approached her table. She was so busy examining his face that she failed to notice the single red rose he held in his hand.

"Hey, sweetheart. Sorry I'm late." He handed her the rose.

"Oh, thank you." She felt a blush. "That's very sweet of you." She placed the stem carefully next to her silverware. Her heart increased its thumping. She really did like him. Life could be so cruel.

He took his seat, and the server approached with another menu in hand. As she passed it to him, Macy took a deep breath, unsure if she should start with an apology for their last fight, or let him bring up the subject. It wasn't totally her fault, but she felt sure an apology for her part in the disagreement was in order.

Troy shifted in his seat a bit and leaned toward her. "I owe you an apology. I never should have pressured you to go to that party. I'm so sorry, Macy." The regret in his voice was clear.

"It's okay. I'm sorry too. I should have tried a little harder. It's unfair for me to expect you to always make concessions for my issues." She chewed the inside of her lip for a moment. "I just worry that we will never find that common ground, you know?"

He shook his head. "You weren't ready for a crowd that size. And I didn't know the hostess was going to have lit candles everywhere. You tried to tell me. I was the one that was in the wrong."

"But that doesn't mean you shouldn't go without me."

Macy sighed. "You can't rearrange your entire social schedule around me, Troy."

He reached across the table and took her hand in his. "I really like you, Macy, and I want to be with you. I don't mind skipping a few parties or whatever. It's not that big a deal."

She felt heat rush to her cheeks again, and that flutter in her chest picked up speed. "I care about you too. So much so that I don't want you to resent me down the road over things you've missed out on because of me. It's why I left you there, hoping you'd have fun despite my panic attack."

He gave her hand a squeeze. "That's not gonna happen. I could never resent you. Ever. I'm in this for the long haul."

The server arrived, interrupting anything Macy would have said in reply.

She filled their waters and took their order, which gave Macy a few seconds to contemplate her next words. "Troy, I appreciate you so much. You've stood beside me when I needed you most. I don't have many people I can depend on. But I have no idea where this is all going. With my condition, things can get complicated. They have gotten complicated. The triggers, the inability to function in public at times." She inhaled deeply. ".... I don't even want to be with myself sometimes. I will not hold you to any commitments." She blew out a breath of frustration and watched his reaction with concern. She wasn't sure she could make anyone normal understand what it's like to be in her head. Life with her would probably always be chaotic and unpredictable in the worst of ways.

Troy reached across the table and took her hands in his. "Complicated doesn't scare me."

"Does crazy?" She blurted out.

He gave her hands a squeeze. "You are not crazy, Macy

McCall. You're beautiful, smart, funny, and talented. If anyone at this table is crazy, it's me. I'm crazy over you."

Macy stared at him a moment, her lips pressed together tightly. Then laughter bubbled up from some absurd place in her brain. She slapped her hand over her mouth to stop it, but the reaction refused to be denied. She quietly shook, her shoulders bouncing up and down as she did her best not to make a scene.

Troy sat back and crossed his arms. "You're laughing at me."

She shook her head, but couldn't look him in the eye.

"Okay, I deserve that. That last line was pretty cheesy." A grin spread across his face and soon he was laughing along with her.

She took a moment to catch her breath and glanced at the surrounding tables. No one was staring or looking at them oddly. She hoped she'd actually managed to seem normal for a few minutes. She rarely felt as if she fit in with the world around her, but other diners who were also chatting and laughing and enjoying their meals surrounded them. Just as she and Troy were.

She reached for his hand once more. "You are a treasure, Troy Stevens. I don't deserve you."

"You're right." He sighed. "You deserve so much better. But I'm not willing to give you up, so if better comes along he should be prepared to fight for you."

Tears filled her eyes. "No, you deserve better than me, but if you're willing to put up with my chaos, I'll happily do my best to make it work."

He leaned across the table and gently kissed her lips. "That's all I ask."

The server brought their food, and they spent the rest of their meal keeping the conversation light and simple.

She studied Troy's face as he talked animatedly about the latest book he was reading, and she relaxed. Maybe, just maybe, they did have a future together.

It was a few minutes after 9:00 p.m. when Macy unlocked the door to her house and slipped inside. Troy was right on her heels.

"Can't I stay for just a bit? You've never let me come in before." He kissed her forehead.

Macy hesitated, then smiled. "Sure, but not too long. I have to start on a new commission early in the morning."

She quickly locked the deadbolt behind him as he entered the foyer.

A long whistle escaped his lips. "Damn. This place is enormous. You live here by yourself?"

She nodded as she flipped on a lamp that added to her already well-lit home. "For now. I have a cleaning lady once a week and my uncle stops by occasionally to see how I'm getting on."

"So this place was your parents' first?" He followed her into a large living area as she again turned on several lights that would seem excessive to most people.

"Yes, and no. The land was theirs, but this house is new. There weren't enough stable parts of the old house to salvage. It's just a shell on the other end of the property." She sat on a large leather sofa. "My uncle had this house built. It's too big for me, but my uncle has always been grandiose in everything he does. He lived here and raised me after my parents…" she sighed. "He didn't want to rebuild in the old spot. Neither of us wanted that reminder."

Troy nodded in appreciation as he took a stroll around the

room. "He did a magnificent job. This place is amazing." As if an afterthought, he added. "And yeah, I get why you'd want to avoid the other house."

"Thank you." She replied quietly. Her mood dampened a bit at the thought of her old home. She didn't like to remember it. None of her recent memories were pleasant.

Troy sat beside her. "Sorry if I'm picking at old wounds. I don't mean to. I'm just a little curious. There's so much you still haven't told me." He reached for her hand and lightly pressed his lips into her palm. "You'll tell me if I'm getting too nosey, right?"

Macy moved her gaze to his. "I will. I promise."

He smiled and put an arm around her, pulling her back against the sofa with him. She laid her head on his chest and closed her eyes. His fingers traced tiny circles on her back as he held her. It was hypnotizing. She snuggled closer to him and enjoyed the warmth of his body against hers.

"This is nice." She murmured.

"Mmm, it is." he answered.

Her mind drifted to thoughts of the future. A future they might have together. She was making so much progress with Dr. Yates. He believed she could achieve a semblance of normal in time. That's all she'd ever wanted.

As she breathed slowly and deeply, her thoughts shifted to her old home once more. Something urgent nagged at her subconscious and electricity pulsed through her veins as panic caused her to open her eyes. It was unusually bright and hot. She sat up and rubbed her face. Her vision cleared and she could make out shadowed figures on the other side of the room. In moments, smoke filled the entire living area. She coughed and choked, reaching for Troy, but she couldn't find him.

"Troy!" Her shout pitched with terror.

No answer. She felt for him next to her, but he was no longer on the sofa.

She crawled on her hands and knees.

"Troy! Where are you?"

All was silent except for the crackle of flames.

"No God, please. Not again." She cried.

Then she heard her name, faint and slightly unfamiliar. As if it were more a memory than an actual voice. It floated toward her through the dark swirls of ash and smoke.

"Macy, come here. I'll get you out."

She couldn't place the voice, yet she felt sure she knew it.

"This way, Macy. Follow my voice."

She crawled toward where she thought the shouts were coming from, but she couldn't get oriented and the words echoed around her.

"Macy, sweetie! Come quick!"

Macy froze, her voice refusing to work. Tears streamed down her face just as she mustered some volume. "Daddy!" She shouted as she closed her eyes and reached out in front of her.

"Where are you, Daddy? I can't find you!" Her voice shook with fear.

"Macy! Macy, wake up!" She heard Troy's voice and felt hands on her shoulders, shaking her softly.

She squirmed away from him, her eyes flying open. "What?"

"You were having a nightmare." Troy's eyes were wide and his hands continued to reach for her.

She rubbed her face and felt the tears that covered her cheeks. Macy jumped up from the sofa and looked around the room. All was as it had been when they'd arrived earlier.

"I was dreaming?" She ran her fingers through her hair,

pulling a barrette out of place. It slid down the side of her head, hanging from the few stray stands it still clung to.

Troy stood and moved to be next to her. "Are you okay? You were asking for your dad." His eyes searched her face and she could see he was trying not to touch her again.

"No, I'm fine. Thank you. I just… sometimes I have bad dreams."

He frowned. "You must have been tired. You fell asleep quickly. Do you have nightmares often? You've never talked about them."

She placed a hand on his arm. "I am tired. Things have been a little stressful lately. But I'll be okay. I just need to get some proper sleep." She kissed his cheek. "Can we talk tomorrow? I should go to bed."

Troy pulled her in for a hug and held on tight. "Yes, tomorrow is fine. I'm here for you, Macy. Anytime, day or night. Please don't forget that." He paused. "I could stay, if you want me to. Nothing intimate, just let me be here for you."

She smiled as her face pressed against his chest and she wrapped her arms around his waist. "I appreciate it, but I'll be fine. I promise to call if I need you."

He pulled back from the hug and kissed her gently on the lips. She showed him to the door, taking a moment to unlock it.

"Drive safe." She whispered.

Troy winked at her. "Always do. Goodnight."

"Night." She shut the door behind him and turned the lock as quickly as she could. Her back pressed against it as she worked to calm her thoughts before they morphed into a crying jag. She wanted him to stay, but she wasn't ready for that step, intimacy or not.

Macy closed her eyes and concentrated on her accomplishments. They'd went out on another date. She ate at a somewhat busy restaurant. She even allowed him to come inside her home. That was a big step for her. Macy rarely let anyone she hadn't known for years inside her fortress of safety. She was making progress, and she needed to acknowledge that, even if it felt like she also suffered setbacks.

She grabbed her purse from the side table next to the door, then slipped off her shoes and carried them upstairs to her bedroom. As always, her bedside lamp was on and as she walked through the door, she flicked the overhead light switch on as well. She didn't sleep well with the lights on all the time, but she slept even worse with them off. And she'd already had one nightmare tonight before she'd even made it to the bed.

Macy pulled her blue cotton dress over her head and tossed it on a nearby chair, then she shuffled into the bathroom to wash her face and brush her teeth. Once she'd completed her nightly bedtime ritual, she took off her bra and pantyhose, then slipped into a large t-shirt and shorts. She looked down at the t-shirt and scoffed. It was an old Maroon 5 concert tee that someone had gifted her several years ago. She loved to pretend she'd bought it herself while attending such a big event. The truth was so much more depressing. She'd never been to a concert in her life. Maybe that would change now that Dr. Yates was treating her. She smiled at the thought of him. He always kept things professional, but he was very kind, and she felt he had the most caring heart of anyone she'd ever met. And if she were honest, she had to admit to having a small crush on him. But she knew it was superficial and nothing like the feelings she had for Troy. Gratitude and affection could sometimes become mangled in her head, so she knew it was nothing she'd ever act on.

Macy stretched and noticed a twisted slat on her blinds.

She walked to the window to adjust it when something caught her eye on the driveway below. She was on the second floor, and the security lights usually made everything below easy to see, but as she peered down at the perfectly smooth concrete she once again caught a flash of something mostly indistinguishable. Deep down, she knew what it was.

Macy stepped back from the window. Her heart pounded like a drum and she could hear the blood rushing in her ears. With all the courage she could gather, she forced herself to look out the window once more. Below, just at the edge of the lighted drive, was a slim figure. She stepped forward, allowing the light to fall on her. Her face tilted up to Macy's bedroom window as if she knew Macy was watching. The figure's blue dress a replica of the one Macy wore tonight.

Macy tore her eyes from the driveway long enough to check the chair she'd tossed her clothes on. Her dress was still there. In a panic, she grabbed the cord on the blinds and yanked them up, hoping to get a better look. The figure stood there, immobile. She couldn't see all of her face, but she knew. It was her twin. Her doppelgänger. She'd never seen her near her home before. The other times were always out in public.

It had to be a hallucination. There was no other explanation. She released the cord, and the blinds crashed to the windowsill in a clatter.

Macy hurried to the bathroom and got a small glass of water, then fumbled for her medication and popped the lid. Her hands were shaking so badly that she spilled a couple of pills on the floor before landing one in her palm. Swiftly, she downed the pill and the water. Kneeling, she picked up the stray capsules from the floor and placed them back inside the bottle. With the lid back on securely, she crawled to the side of her bed and placed the pill bottle on the nightstand.

Macy leaned herself against the side of the bed and put her head against her knees. "You're being an idiot, Macy." She whispered out loud. "It's impossible for her to be real. It's just in your head."

She blew out a long, steady breath and closed her eyes. "The checklist." She muttered.

A frown formed as she realized she couldn't use the most important parts of the list. *Can anyone else see it? Can anyone else hear it?* She had no one to ask those questions to at the moment. As much as she hated it, there was only one question on the list she could really answer, did she feel in danger? Hell yes, she did. This terrified her.

Her eyes shifted to her bedroom door, and she thought she saw a shadow pass under it. In seconds she was at the door and locked the knob. Staggering backward, she landed on the bed. She didn't take her eyes off the door as she climbed under the blankets and pulled them up to her chin.

She spent the rest of the night staring at the door, fighting to stay awake as she waited for a specter that never showed.

4

MACY

Macy stared at the blank canvas in front of her. Her eyes wouldn't focus properly.

"Shit." She groaned as she tossed her paintbrush on the table. "I need coffee."

Macy's bare feet padded down the hall until she reached the kitchen. A yawn escaped her lips as she filled the carafe and poured it into the water reservoir.

"Yeah, gonna need the entire pot today." She muttered to herself.

She put the carafe in place, added the coffee and pushed the start button. Her chin rested on her hands as she leaned down to watch the dark liquid slowly fill the pot.

"Faster, please. I need to work today." She instructed the machine through another yawn.

Macy grabbed her favorite mug and inspected it closely. The colors faded, and the glaze began showing signs of age. Her father gave her that mug, and it meant the world to her. One side had a big heart, the other side had cursive writing proclaiming her *World's Best Daughter*. He'd surprised her with it on her ninth birthday. "Now you can drink morning

Joe like the grown-ups" he'd proclaimed proudly. She'd frowned and asked him why anyone would want to drink someone named Joe.

He'd laughed so hard at that, and she didn't understand the joke at first, until her mother explained that Joe was another name for coffee. It was one of those happier memories that'd stuck with her.

Then there was the day the housekeeper, Miss Christy, accidentally dropped it and broke the handle. Macy was heartbroken, but Miss Christy assured her it was fixable.

Macy ran her finger over the crack that still showed, thankful it had survived the fire. Miss Christy was another happy memory.

Because of her father's crazy schedule, Macy didn't get out of the house a lot as a child, but Miss Christy had a daughter about her age named Brandy, and they'd played often. She made sure Macy was never lonely. They did their lessons together, and Brandy was the closest thing she'd ever had to a best friend.

Macy swallowed hard as she envisioned the last time she saw them. Miss Christy's face was full of terror. She coughed and clung to Brandy while screaming for help from a second-floor window.

Macy pushed away the guilt, reciting her affirmations in her head, and filled her cup with liquid inspiration before heading back to the room that was her art studio.

Her cell phone rang, and she hit the speaker button.

"Hello?" She answered as she dipped her brush in red acrylic.

"Hey Macy, it's Uncle Robbie. How are you doing, ladybug?" His baritone voice always soothed her nerves. She needed a little calm after last night. His use of her nickname also made her smile. He'd started calling her that when she was two years old because of her fascination with all things ladybug.

"I'm okay. Tired." She swirled the brush on the bright white canvas.

"Nightmares?" He inquired.

"No, just… didn't sleep well." She hadn't told him about seeing her doppelgänger. It wasn't something she wanted to admit to herself, let alone anyone else. So far, only Dr. Yates knew about that.

"Do you need to take those sleeping pills again?" Concern laced his words.

"No, I'll be fine. Just the occasional bad night. You know how it is." She dipped her brush in the red and made another broad stroke.

He didn't reply for a moment, and she'd feared he'd hung up. "Uncle?"

"I'm here. I was just thinking. Maybe I should come stay for a few days. I can get enough work done here to take some time off, and I don't have any dates on the docket until next week."

"I'm fine. Seriously." She placed her brush on the palette and carefully sat them on the table next to her.

"I worry about you out there all by yourself." He stated.

"I'm not a child anymore, Uncle Robbie. I'm twenty-four and doing okay on my own." She hoped she didn't sound like a spoiled child.

"I know, ladybug, but with your condition-"

She cut him off. "I'm on medication and have amazing doctors. I'm good." She tried changing the subject. "Troy came over last night."

"You let him come in the house?" Robert's voice gave away his surprise.

"Yes. We sat on the sofa and talked a while, then he went

home and I went to bed. It was nice." She wasn't lying about it being nice, but she would not bring up the negative experiences of the evening.

"Glad to hear it. That's progress." She could almost hear his smile.

"See?" She smirked. "I'm practically cured."

He laughed. "Okay, smartass, I'll give you your space. But don't forget your lonely Uncle Robbie will be eating dinners alone in his office and worrying about you now and then."

"Right." She rolled her eyes. "Because that's all you have to do is worry about me."

"Okay, so maybe I'll be working too. But just because I'm preoccupied doesn't mean I won't think about you."

She laughed. "I'd hope so. Oh, by the way, please tell Mrs. Chase that I'm working on her painting now and should have it done soon. Two weeks at most, I'd think, if the muse cooperates."

"She'll be glad to hear it. She's been dying to tell her friends she has a Macy McCall original in her foyer."

Macy shook her head. "Well, she's paying a shit-load for it, so she can tell people whatever she wants."

"That's the spirit. Screw passion, give me the cash." He said.

She laughed once more. "Okay, old man. I gotta work. I'll call you later in the week, okay?"

"Sounds good. Love you, ladybug."

"Love you too, Uncle. Later." She hit end and turned to look at her work so far. She didn't know what it would end up being, but she always let her emotions lead her creativity. So far it hadn't failed her. Random shapes and colors would always end up in a combination that resembled something recognizable, mostly. It wasn't always super obvious, but usually enough that people felt moved by it. Her paintings had sold for hundreds, sometimes thousands among the elite in her area. Something about her mixture of colors and textures drew in art fanatics like flies. And while she didn't always understand it, she would not complain. The money from her work allowed her to cover her living expenses without having to touch the money her parents had left her. It also allowed her to donate to various humanitarian efforts that were dear to her.

Macy picked up her brush and began working again, letting her heart guide her hand. When her muse took over, she'd zone out a bit while she worked. Her uncle once compared it to watching someone have an out-of-body-experience. She was there, but only subconsciously. As if her body was being run by some invisible force as she splashed colors on the canvas.

Dr. Yates was happy to hear she was painting. He reminded her it was great therapy, and she had to agree. Some of her best work came after her worst moments. Moments like last night.

"This one had better become a fucking masterpiece" she muttered to herself as she worked. She never wanted to experience a night like that again. Not even to paint something amazing.

Two hours had passed when she realized her hands were cramping. She placed her brushes on the table and stretched. The clock on the wall reminded her it was nearing lunchtime. She'd take a break, eat a light lunch, and then get back to it.

She studied the canvas and frowned. "Where am I going with this?"

It didn't yet have much of a recognizable shape. Just various bold colors streaked across the entire canvas with some forming a large box. She pulled open a drawer to grab a new tube of white and didn't see what she needed. Macy jerked another drawer open as she rummaged through her tubes of paint.

"Shit!" She needed white to mix colors. She couldn't go any further without it.

She picked up her phone, intending to call for delivery, then stopped herself. Dr. Yates said she needed to get out more. He said she should make quick trips, building up her comfort level with each venture.

Determined to make this work, she called for her regular driver, then ran upstairs to change out of her painting clothes and run a brush through her hair. Once she felt sure she was presentable, she grabbed her purse and waited near the door for Jenn to arrive.

Jenn was a friendly woman that Macy had met through her uncle, and she had offered to help Macy with her transportation needs. She was the only person Macy was comfortable riding with. Jenn worked as a server, but helped Macy out on her off days and on lunch breaks. That meant sometimes she had to wait until Jenn was available, but she didn't care. She'd rather stay home before she rode with someone she didn't know at a cab company. Macy paid her well, so Jenn was happy to accommodate Macy whenever possible. Even when it meant driving several miles out of town to pick her up and bring her back home.

Jenn usually dropped Macy off for her weekly appointments with Dr. Yates. Then Macy would ride the bus to her Uncle's office and he'd drive her home once his day was complete. It wasn't always the fastest way home, but it worked for her. It also allowed her to see her uncle at least once a week so they could catch up on things.

Jenn pulled up and Macy quickly locked up behind her before jumping in the back seat.

"Hey girlie! How are you today?" Jenn's cheerful voice floated to the back seat where Macy preferred to ride. "I'm good, you?" Macy buckled.

"I'm hanging in there. Where we off to today?" Jenn's long, slender fingers opened her GPS system on her phone.

"I need to go to that big art supply store. The one on Kingsbury." Macy dug money out of her wallet.

"You got it." Jenn punched in the address and pulled out of the drive. As they neared the street, Macy couldn't help but look at the spot where she'd seen her body double. Nothing was there, but a chill ran down her spine just the same.

Macy watched the scenery fly by until they reached the art store. Jenn was great about not expecting small talk. She only took part in a conversation if Macy started it. Otherwise, she gave Macy peace during their trips. It was something that Macy appreciated about Jenn. She knew little about Macy's disorder, but she never pried and seemed to grasp that talking was sometimes the last thing she needed.

"Here ya go." Jenn pulled up to the curb. "Do you need me to wait or come back in a bit?"

"If you can come back, I won't be too long." Macy replied as she passed some cash over the seat.

"Happy to. I'll go grab some lunch and be back in a few." Jenn flipped through her phone after accepting the money. "You're too good to me, girlie. See you soon."

Macy climbed out and shut the door, staring up at the enormous building before her. She squared her shoulders and steeled her nerves. "I can do this. It's just a few people in an art store. Nothing too confined. No open flames. Noise level should be tolerable. Easy." Her stomach was doing flips, but she tried to ignore it.

Macy pulled open the door and quickly stepped inside. She'd been in there many times before, but she'd always been with someone else. Someone to support her when her panic got the better of her.

This part of her illness really frustrated her. She could be so confident when she was in familiar, safe spaces, like her home. But out in public, she became a timid wreck. It was almost like she was two different people in those situations, and she hated it.

Macy grabbed a small basket and quickly navigated the aisles. She wanted to get what she needed and get out. The crowd was fairly small, but the store was too busy for her liking. The noises of the other patrons seemed to surround her, forming a claustrophobic bubble that made her every movement difficult. She breathed in and out slowly. The music felt louder than normal. When she opened her eyes, she noticed a large man walking toward her. She picked up a tube of white and inspected it to assure it was the right brand. The closer he came, the smaller she felt. She knew it made no sense, but she couldn't help it. Her panic set in and she grabbed several tubes and power walked farther down the aisle, taking the corner almost at a jogger's pace. To be safe, she grabbed a pack of bright colors on her way to the register as well. She didn't want to make a return trip anytime soon.

Once she reached the checkout, she had to wait behind two other customers. One was buying brushes and quickly left. The elderly lady in front of her took longer.

"Can you tell me if these pigment sticks are the ones on sale? I found them on that third aisle, but someone had scattered the different brands all over the shelf." The woman smiled at the cashier and the young man returned her smile.

"Sure, let me check on that for you." He picked up a sale flier, but Macy didn't hear what he said next.

Her focus was solely on the woman standing just outside the glass doors. The woman wore a pair of jeans, a blue t-shirt, and had her brown hair up in a messy bun. It mimicked her own look perfectly. Her eyes landed on Macy and she smiled.

Macy gripped the basket and felt a shard of the thin plastic handle dig deep into her skin. In response to the pain, she dropped it. The woman in front of her turned to face her.

Macy crouched down to pick up the paint tubes that had spilled out onto the floor.

"Are you okay?" The customer in front of her flashed a friendly smile.

"Ah, uh, yes. Thank you." Not wanting to miss an opportunity, she pointed to the glass door. "Do you see that woman?"

The woman turned her face to the glass just as Macy got another good look. The Macy-look-alike vanished.

She ran her hand down her face. "But…"

The cashier and customer both looked at her with concern.

Macy momentarily wrestled with her need to know the truth and her fear. It terrified her to seek out her doppelgänger, but she no longer wanted to live in fear of her either. In a moment of rare clarity and bravery, truth won out, and she felt just enough courage to go after this apparition that haunted her. "I'll be right back." Macy put the basket on the counter and dashed out the front door.

She could hear the blood rushing through her veins and her vision became a little blurry as her anxiety once again fought for control. Her head whipped back and forth, frantically searching for the woman. She glimpsed the shirt and hair that she was sure belonged to her double.

Macy ran down the sidewalk, all her normal fears pushed aside in a surge of adrenaline as she sought validation. She had to know if this was real or a hallucination. She had to know if she was losing her mind.

The blue-shirted woman turned a corner, and Macy did her best to catch up. Once she reached the corner, she saw the woman enter a small convenience store. A small space.

"Dammit!" She took a moment to breathe. Nausea plagued her.

Macy followed, her heart pounding in her chest and her feet feeling heavier and heavier with each step. She once more saw the flash of the blue shirt as it entered the ladies' room. Another small room. Macy approached, then stood outside the door, working up her nerve to enter. After a moment, she cautiously opened the door and stepped inside. Her eyes scanned the area for her twin, but she was completely alone. The stalls were empty, doors wide open.

Macy pushed out a shaky breath and grabbed a paper towel. She ran cold water over it, rang it out, and patted the back of her neck as she leaned over the sink. She focused on her breathing exercises.

"Looking for me?" It came as a soft whisper from behind her.

Macy froze and lifted her gaze to the mirror. Her double was only a few steps behind her.

"Who are you?" Macy managed to get the words out without screaming them, but she gripped the sink as if it were the only thing holding her upright.

The woman smiled. "I'm you."

Macy shook her head. "No, it's not possible."

"Why do you say that? It's very possible. Especially with

someone as screwed up as you." The woman smirked, and she laced her last sentence with venom.

"Why? Why am I seeing you?" Macy's voice broke.

"Because you are racked with guilt. What you did is unforgivable."

Macy closed her eyes. "No." She whispered. "No, that's not true." She placed the damp paper towel against her face. "Go away. You're not real."

The voice was next to her ear now. "Oh, but I'm real enough. I exist in your head and I'm going to make you pay."

Macy dropped the paper towel and gripped the sink once more to keep from collapsing to the floor. She was afraid to open her eyes. She didn't want to see the hatred she knew would burn in the eyes of her double.

All was deathly quiet for a moment more, then the bathroom door swung open and a little girl rushed in. Macy turned to watch the girl slam a stall door, then fiddle with the lock on the other side.

Macy inspected her surroundings but saw no one else.

She turned back to the faucet and splashed water on her face, then released a small laugh. She was losing her marbles. Completely, without a doubt, losing it.

5

MACY

The sidewalk Macy walked on seemed unstable and much longer than she remembered. The art supply store should be in her view at any moment, and yet she wasn't seeing it.

She leaned against a brick wall as others quickly passed. The blur of people and cars was swirling together. She could hear her heartbeat above all the noise of the city. Beads of sweat rolled down her face.

Macy slid down the wall and pulled her knees to her chest. "Breathe. Breathe." She reminded herself. "It wasn't real. None of that was real."

"Hey, are you okay, lady?" A teen kneeled in front of her, his face barely in focus. "Do you need some help?"

She shook her head. She just wanted to be left alone.

"Okay, then." He stood and walked away.

Macy buried her head in her knees. With closed eyes, she silently begged her thoughts to calm. At that moment, everything was rushing around in her mind at once. Being bombarded with so much overwhelmed her and she would often shut down in these moments. This time was no different.

She didn't know how long she'd been there before Dr. Yates' voice echoed in her ears. "Do you need some help?"

She shook her head, trying to clear the hallucination.

A hand touched her shoulder. "Macy? Is that you? It's me. Dr. Yates."

She raised her face to his. "Is it really you?"

He smiled. "It is. Why are you sitting here alone?"

She shook her head. "I… I can't seem to move."

He reached out a hand. "Let me help you."

She gingerly reached for him, terrified that her touch would make him disappear into thin air. A warm grip surrounded hers and she sighed in relief.

Dr. Yates slowly pulled her to her feet. "What happened?"

Macy wrapped her arms around herself in a gesture of protection. Her mind was clearing, and she credited that to her favorite doctor standing before her. "I… I saw her."

He nodded. "Okay. I take it you didn't have a pleasant experience."

Macy shook her head. "No, I didn't."

"Were you heading somewhere? Do you need a ride?"

She turned to look around, trying to remember why she'd come into town. Her other memories slowly came into focus. "Oh, yes, paint."

"Paint? For your work?"

She nodded.

A frown creased his brow. "What store were you going to?"

"The store on Kingsbury." She rubbed her arms and looked at those walking past them.

"Are you sure? You're nowhere near there."

She froze. "What? Holy shit! Where am I?"

"Near my office. That's probably the only reason I saw you here." He pulled keys out of his pocket.

Macy looked around and recognized her surroundings. She put her hands over her face. "Oh, God. I'm so sorry. I'm so very sorry." She felt tears roll down her cheeks.

Daniel put a hand on her shoulder. "Do you want me to call someone for you? Troy? Or your Uncle?"

Macy shook her head and wiped her face. "I don't know."

"Do you have your cell phone?" He held out his hand.

She dug her phone out of her pocket, used her passcode to unlock it, and gave it to him.

He scrolled through her contacts and she watched as he called two different numbers.

"No answer." He looked around and sighed. "Well, I can't leave you here. And I know you don't feel safe with strangers, so a cab isn't a good idea. C'mon. I'm not parked too far from here."

She let him guide her for about a block before reaching a parking garage. She stopped. "I don't know if I can go in there."

He looked at the entrance. "I could bring the car out. Will you be okay to wait here?"

She nodded. "I promise not to move from this spot."

He grinned. "Well, you might want to move a little. We're standing in front of the gate."

She chuckled, and it made her feel a tad better. "Okay, I'll move over here," she took a few steps to the left, "and then I won't move."

He smiled. "Excellent choice. I'll be right back."

Macy waited patiently, trying to keep her mind off of her earlier hallucination.

The gate lifted and a yellow Jeep Wrangler pulled out of

the gate and stopped in front of her. The passenger door opened and Dr. Yates leaned across the seat. "Hop in!"

She cautiously approached the vehicle and took a seat. She closed the door and buckled up, then let her eyes take in the vehicle's interior. It was a habit she'd picked up after the fire. She always looked for a viable exit strategy, even when it made little sense. She chalked it up to just another layer of her paranoia.

Dr. Yates was silent for a moment, and she realized he was giving her time to adjust. "I'm ready. Thank you for giving me a minute."

He smiled. "Not a problem. Art store?"

"Yes, please. If it's not too much trouble."

"Not at all." He waited for a couple of cars to pass, then pulled out into the street. The ride was a quiet one. Although he was her therapist, they weren't at one of her sessions and she appreciated he wasn't pushing her to talk about it. She wasn't sure she could, yet. It was still a little fuzzy. She'd had other foggy moments in the past that she hadn't recovered fully. How she got from the bathroom at the convenience store to Dr. Yates' office may always be a mystery.

"Thank you again for the ride. I'm guessing this crosses some kind of patient-doctor line." She was appreciative, no matter what line it may have crossed.

"It's not a big deal, really. It's actually fortunate I was driving today. I don't own a car and usually take a cab. The Jeep belongs to my friend Roger. He had a procedure and isn't supposed to drive, so I'll be picking him up later today." He gave her a side glance. "I'm glad I'm the one that found you, it's always better to see a familiar face." He pulled the Jeep in front of the art supply store and turned off the engine.

Unless it's my own. "Thank you again. I'm sorry to have troubled you." Macy opened the door.

"It's really no trouble. Let me help you get what you need and get you home." Dr. Yates exited the vehicle and jogged around to the sidewalk to meet her.

"You don't have to. I can manage." She shut the door behind her.

"I know you can, but I would feel better if you let me assure you make it home safely." He put his hands in his pockets and smiled down at her.

She nodded her head.

He followed her into the store, and the cashier recognized her immediately. "Hey, it's you. Are you okay?"

She felt heat rise to her cheeks. "I'm fine. Thank you."

"Your friend was looking for you. She asked me to call her if I saw you again." He pulled a card out of his pocket.

"Thank you, that's very kind. I'll call her and let her know I'm okay."

"I still have your basket here. I was going to put the items back after my break, but… if you still want them, they are here." The young man's kindness made her smile.

"Yes. Please." She pulled her wallet out of her pocket.

As he rang the items up, Dr. Yates asked him a question. "Did you see what upset her so much?"

The cashier shook his head. "Sorry, I didn't see anything. She mentioned a woman, but we didn't know what she was talking about."

Macy handed him cash. "I'm sorry for causing a scene."

"No trouble. Just glad you're okay." He smiled and handed her the change.

"Thank you." Replied Dr. Yates. He followed Macy back to his Jeep and opened the door for her. Once she was settled, he returned to the driver's seat and brought the engine to life.

"I know you said it's no big deal, but I do feel bad for interrupting your day. I feel like a fucking moron." She kept her head down and her eyes on her hands. Her habit of cursing when upset did not offend Dr. Yates, and she was thankful for that.

"Nonsense. I have the rest of the day off, so you aren't interrupting anything. You're not a moron, fucking or otherwise." He glanced at her as he turned on to the highway and drove west.

She laughed, and he grinned. "We'll discuss the details at our next appointment, but is there anything you need to tell me now?" He gave her another sidelong glance before moving his focus back to the road.

"You aren't on the clock, Dr. Yates. You don't have to worry about it." Her expression had become stoic again.

"Consider it on the house." He smirked. "Honestly though, if you need to talk at all before I drop you off, I'm happy to listen. We're in this car together for several more minutes. Might as well make it productive, right?"

She shrugged. "It's still a little fuzzy. But I saw her while I was getting supplies. I ran out to talk to her, or maybe confront her, and she disappeared."

His eyebrows rose in surprise. "You went after her? I'm impressed. And you don't remember how you ended up near my office?" He kept his eyes front and center as he spoke.

She nodded. "Correct."

They drove in silence until they reached her house. He pulled down the long circle drive, stopping in front of her door. Once he put the Jeep in park, he turned to face her. "Why do I feel you're leaving something out, Macy?"

"Dr. Yates, you don't have to-"

He held up a hand and cut her off. "I'm not doing anything I don't want to do. While I make a good living, I don't just do this for money. I do it because I genuinely care and want to help people. I want to help you, Macy. But I can only do that if you are one hundred percent honest with me.”

She released a deep sigh. “I followed her into a bathroom.”

His brows knit together in confusion. “A bathroom?”

She nodded. “At a convenience store. I entered the room, and she wasn’t there. Then suddenly she was standing behind me as I faced the sinks.”

“And…” he urged.

“And I asked her who she was.” Macy turned her eyes to his. “She said she was me.”

He pressed his lips together. “Interesting.”

Macy frowned. “She was angry. She said she’d make me pay for what I did.”

“What you did, when?”

Macy’s voice cracked. “The fire.”

Dr. Yates frowned and rubbed the bridge of his nose. “As I’ve suggested, likely a manifestation of your unjustified guilt.”

“It looks that way. But, it felt so real, doctor. I’ve never had a hallucination until her and it was so vivid.” She pulled her keys from her pocket. “I know it can’t be real. I know that. It’s just so confusing. Am I getting worse?”

He shook his head. “No, you’re not. We’ll keep working on it, okay?”

She nodded, opened the door, and slid out. “Thank you. For everything. The talk, the ride, keeping me safe… all of it.”

“It’s my pleasure. Are you going to be okay? Do we need to attempt to call someone again?”

“I’ll be fine. I just need to get back to work. That will help a lot.”

He nodded. “Okay then.”

She shut the door, and hepull down the drive. Macy watched him drive away and her admiration of him heightened.

She quickly let herself inside and locked up behind her. With newly purchased paint in hand, she went back into her studio and set everything back up to resume her work. As she dipped her brush in the white, she found she couldn't keep her hand steady. Her strokes were sloppy and with each attempt she became more and more angry.

"Damn it!" She shouted as she tossed her brush on a nearby table. "Calm down, Macy," she told herself. "You need to channel this energy into your work, not allow it to hinder you."

She hurried upstairs, each step in coordination with a deep breath in and out. Her affirmations repeating in her mind. She reached her bedroom and wasted no time taking her anxiety medication. She stepped into the bathroom and stared into the mirror, expecting to see her other self appear behind her as before. To her relief, this time she only saw her reflection.

6

DANIEL

$\mathcal{D}$aniel walked into his apartment and flopped down on the sofa. Weariness from the afternoon had finally sunk in. His morning had been average, but then he'd found Macy cowering on a sidewalk near his building. She was disoriented, scared, and alone. While there are professional boundaries to be considered, he couldn't just leave her there. And he knew that in that moment, she needed a friend. He felt he needed to be that for her.

But these hallucinations she was having concerned him. It wasn't part of the usual symptoms of her condition. He'd need to consult with some colleagues and her other doctors to understand the cause. But even with apparent indications that these are hallucinations, Macy struggled to distinguish the difference between reality and imagination.

His cell phone rang, and he saw Roger's name on the caller I.D.

"Hey Roger."

"Danny boy! I wanted to thank you again for bringing me home. I was kind of out of it earlier with all the pain meds. I'm more alert now." Roger was overly jubilant.

He sighed, weariness evident in his voice. "I'm happy to help."

"Hey, did you ever call that hottie from the bar the other night?" Daniel could envision Roger's elated expression.

"No, I haven't called her." He rubbed the slight stubble on his chin.

Roger's voice was loud as he said, "Man, what is wrong with you? She was smokin' hot and so into you."

"Roger, listen, I'm not sure I'm ready for another relationship, and you know I'm not into flings."

"You need to move on, my friend. I know you loved Vanessa, but… damn it. You deserve happiness." Roger sighed. "Call Sarah. Take a chance. If it doesn't turn into anything, then you know you gave it a shot and can just say 'hey it was fun'."

Daniel sat in silence for a moment. He thought it over. Roger was right. It'd been ten years. He'd dated a little since she died, but he always compared them to her, and it always sunk their ship before it sailed. As a psychologist, he should know better, but he couldn't seem to stop himself.

"I don't want to over-analyze the mental health of every girl I date." He stood and walked to the kitchen. "You know how I am."

"Shit. Daniel, let that go. It wasn't your fault."

Daniel laughed.

"What's so funny?" Roger asked.

Macy's face flashed in his mind. "It's just ironic. I recently told a patient the same thing. I can't seem to follow my own advice."

"Call. Her. Give it a chance." Roger insisted.

"Okay, okay. I'll do it. Get off my ass."

"About damn time. Call me later and tell me everything." Roger hung up.

Daniel made himself some coffee and went back to the sofa. His head flopped back on the cushion and he closed his eyes. He tried to imagine what he'd say to Sarah.

"Fuck it." He sat up and leaned over to the end table where he'd recently dumped the contents of his pockets. He grabbed Sarah's card and glanced at it.

Sarah Bowman, Acquisitions Editor, Essential Style and Design Magazine.

That impressed him. It sounded like she had a classy job. He smirked as he practiced his speech. "Are you into guys that deal with broken people, who, as it so happens, is a pretty big mess himself?"

Daniel shook his head. Brutal honesty may not win him any points right off the bat.

He picked up his phone and dialed the cell number at the bottom of the card.

After one ring, a sultry, sleepy voice answered. "Hello?"

"Is this Sarah?"

"Yes, this is her." A faint yawn met his ears.

"Did I wake you?" He checked his watch, and it was barely 6:00 p.m.

"No, it's fine. I just dozed off. I needed to get up. Who is this?" He heard her yawn again.

"Oh, sorry. It's Daniel Yates. I met you at The Green Door Tavern a few nights ago." He paused. "I was with the obnoxious bald guy."

She laughed. "I remember you and I'm glad you called. I was beginning to think you didn't want to be my friend after all." He could almost hear a pout in her voice with that last sentence.

"Sorry. I've been a bit busy." He blew out a frustrated breath, his memory jumping back to his latest encounter with Macy. "But I finally had a free minute and thought I'd call."

"I'm glad I merit a free minute." He could hear the sarcasm in her voice.

"Well, I was thinking. If you have more than a few minutes free this week, maybe we could get together." He held his breath, surprised to realize he was nervous.

"I'd like that. I'm free most evenings." She yawned again. "How about tomorrow night?"

"I may not be able to get away from the office early tomorrow, but would Friday work?" He hoped he wasn't blowing it. It'd been a while since he'd asked anyone out.

"Actually," the sound of shuffling papers could be heard before her next reply. "I think Friday would be even better. Do you like Brazilian steakhouses? I've been dying to try that place on Illinois Street."

"That sounds great. Would you like me to pick you up?" He smiled and was sure she could hear it in his voice.

"I'll meet you there, say seven?" Her voice was melodic.

"I'll see you at seven."

She chuckled. "Can't wait. See you soon."

The phone went silent, and he placed it on the table next to him.

"Holy shit. I have a date."

Friday night Daniel sat at a table near the window and sipped his water. Sarah was a few minutes late, and he hoped she hadn't changed her mind. He watched the happy couples around him as they enjoyed each other's company. Maybe someday he'd have that again. Possibly with Sarah.

"Hey, sorry I'm late." She stood in front of him, looking like a goddess.

"No, it's fine." He stood and moved to hold out her chair for her.

"Such a gentleman. Thank you." She smiled widely as she took her seat.

He went back to his own chair and returned her smile. "You look beautiful."

She looked down at the gold v-neck dress she'd chosen for the evening. "Thank you. I wasn't sure how formal this place was, but I think I made the right choice."

He nodded. "I would imagine you'd look amazing in anything you wore."

She tilted her head at him and smirked. "You are a charmer. I'm not a big fan of false flattery, but I'll allow it this once."

Daniel shook his head. "I've not spoken a single untruth. You are a beautiful woman and I'm a lucky man. Tonight I'm the envy of every man in this restaurant."

She blushed. "I don't know. I'm thinking I might be the lucky one. Smart, handsome, successful, sweet… what more could a girl ask for?"

He chuckled and raised his water glass. "To being lucky."

She raised her empty glass. "I don't actually believe in luck, but I'll toast to the sentiment, once someone fills my water."

The server arrived at that moment and filled Sarah's water glass. "Good evening. My name is Cindy and I'll be serving you tonight. Can I start you off with something from the bar?"

Sarah smiled. "I'll have a port, please."

"And I'll have a gin and tonic, please." He spoke to the server, but couldn't tear his eyes from Sarah.

"Got it. I'll bring those right back. While you're waiting,

I'll let you look over the menus." She placed a menu in front of each of them before leaving to get their drinks.

"I don't really believe in luck either, but it sounds good in theory. You mentioned I was successful," Daniel said. "How do you know that?"

Sarah shrugged. "I like to do my homework. You don't think I just go out with any hot guy I see in a bar, do you? I like to at least know that he's gainfully employed and doesn't have any warrants."

He chuckled. "So you did a background check?"

"Well, it wasn't anything that formal. I mostly just looked you up on the internet." She sighed dramatically. "Sadly, I couldn't find any dirt on you, so I have nothing to hold over you."

"Ah, it's good to know the internet hasn't gotten ahold of my secrets yet." He took another sip of water.

The server gave them their drinks and took their orders. Once she left, Sarah cleared her throat.

"I did read something about an accident." Her face was somber.

Daniel stared at her.

"Sorry, I didn't mean to bring up terrible memories."

He shook his head. "No, it's okay. It's just… difficult."

She took a sip of her drink. "Do you want to talk about it?"

"There's not much to talk about." He picked up his glass. "My fiancé Vanessa and I were in her car. It was raining. She was driving. She missed a turn, and we hit a tree." He gulped a large portion of the glass. "I lived. She didn't."

"I'm so sorry." Sarah's voice was low.

Daniel shrugged. "I'm not gonna say that I'm over it, but I can tell you I've accepted it."

"Is that how you hurt your leg?" She glanced at his cane

leaning against the table.

He nodded.

She reached across the table and placed her hand over his. "Well, I'm not in your line of work, but if you ever need an ear, I'm happy to listen."

"Thank you." He finished his drink.

"Now, enough about me. Let's talk about you. Any skeletons in your closet I should know about?" He smiled.

"You didn't check up on me?" She took another drink.

"No. Unlike you, I prefer a little mystery."

She laughed loudly. "Oh my. Then you just hit the jackpot, my friend." She winked at him.

"So, do I have to torture it out of you? Or are you going to at least share a little about yourself?" He teased.

"Hmm…" she examined him for a moment, her expression serious. "I don't know. I might enjoy a little torture if it came from you."

The food arrived and Daniel decided the rest of that conversation was better saved for a more private setting.

Once the server had filled their plates, they ate in silence.

Daniel looked up from his meal and froze.

Sarah frowned. "Are you okay?"

He swallowed the bite he'd just taken. "Yes, just… see someone I know."

"Dr. Yates." Macy's boyfriend Troy waved as he approached their table, Macy walked just behind him, her hand in his.

Daniel stood and shook his free hand. "Troy, it's good to see you again." He turned his attention to Macy. "How are you, Macy?"

She nodded. "I'm good. Thank you again for your help the other day."

Troy pulled her close to him. "Yes, thank you, doctor. I

hate that you couldn't get ahold of me, but I appreciate you took good care of her."

"It was my pleasure." Daniel caught Sarah's curious stare from the corner of his eye. "Oh, so sorry. Where are my manners? Troy and Macy, this is my date, Sarah. Sarah, this is Troy and Macy."

Sarah stood and shook both their hands. "It's nice to meet you. I haven't known Daniel long, but I feel confident in saying you've got a good doctor here."

Macy smiled. "I couldn't agree more."

Daniel's eyes darted from Sarah to Macy.

Daniel noticed Macy fidgeting with her bracelet. He knew that was one of her nervous habits. He realized she wasn't entirely comfortable, either surrounded by so many people or meeting someone new, but she was coping. "Have you gotten your table yet?"

Troy nodded. "We've just finished dinner. We were thinking of seeing a movie."

Sarah smiled. "That sounds fun. Which one?"

Macy cleared her throat. "Oh, we'll grab something from his DVD library. Or mine. I don't really like movie theaters."

Daniel nodded. "Sounds like a wonderful idea. I hope you enjoy the rest of your night."

Troy laced his fingers through Macy's once more. "Will do. And the same to you. It was nice to meet you, Sarah."

"It was wonderful meeting you both." She smiled.

Macy waved as Troy gently urged her along. Daniel waited until Sarah took her seat, then he seated himself.

"Sorry about that." He finished the rest of his drink.

"No, please don't apologize. I'd imagine you run into your patients now and then. She seemed nice."

He sighed. "She is. They both are. How did you know she was a patient?"

"He called you Dr. Yates. Friends rarely address each other that way, and he said you helped her, so I just put two and two together."

He nodded, feeling foolish that her observation had alarmed him. "That makes sense. Thank you for being kind. Sometimes people don't understand just how remarkable my patients are."

"Remarkable?" She smiled at him. "How do you mean?"

"Some have minor things they need to discuss, others have survived trauma we could only imagine in our worst nightmares. Yet they are all brave, wonderful, and very often creative souls who just need to be given a chance to rediscover their happiest selves."

Sarah stared down at her plate for a moment as if lost in thought, then looked back up at Daniel. "That's... the most amazing thing I've ever heard a doctor say." She inhaled a deep breath, then exhaled. "It's obvious you care deeply about helping your patients. I could have used a doctor like you in my youth. It does my heart good to know that men like you exist."

He smiled at her, his joy at her praise reaching a place he felt had been dormant for years. "Thank you. I consider that high praise."

"It is. I'm not a big fan of most doctors, to be honest." She swirled the last of her port in her glass. "But I've not only stumbled on to a compassionate doctor, but an amazing man that I can honestly say I'm proud to be here with tonight."

He felt a bit like an idiot, knowing he had a silly grin on his face as he looked at her. But he couldn't help himself. She was beautiful, smart, funny, and she seemed to genuinely like him. He was starting to think maybe he believed in luck after all.

7

MACY

Macy awoke. Something, or someone, was in her room. When she opened her eyes, she tried to focus. Her bedroom was enveloped in complete darkness. She'd always slept with the small lamp by her bed turned on, so she immediately panicked. When she reached for the lamp, she couldn't find it.

A voice from the darkness taunted her.

"You don't deserve light. You don't deserve fresh air. You deserve nothing you have."

Macy sat up, clutching the covers to her chest. She couldn't move. Terror kept her a prisoner as she tried to make sense of what was happening. *Was this another dream? Was this real?* She couldn't tell anymore.

"When I'm done with you," the voice whispered, this time closer to her face, "you'll wish for a swift death." A light chuckle followed. "And I just might give it to you."

Macy was able to force her arm to move enough to find her phone on the nightstand. She tapped the screen, hoping for any sliver of light. It powered on and illuminated her double's face directly in front of her.

Macy screamed, and the double backed out of the light.

Macy couldn't seem to stop screaming now that she'd started. Her voice a shrill siren in the dark. Fear was hitting her, wave after wave keeping her from breathing properly. She scrambled to get away, but only ended up backed up against her headboard, no closer to safety than she had been before.

Loud laughing filled the room. "No one can hear you out here, Macy. Not too wise to live on all this land by yourself. It actually seems kind of foolish for someone with all your paranoia."

Macy was full on hyperventilating now and trying to focus on restoring oxygen to her lungs.

"You are a mess, aren't you? All the way out here by yourself. Anything could happen."

The doppelgänger flicked on the closet light, her shadowed form filling the doorway. She held up something that, despite being back lit, was obviously a rope with a noose tied at one end. "Anything can happen when someone is as disturbed as you are."

Macy gripped the mattress, her fingernails digging into the fabric. "No! You will not convince me to do that!"

Macy saw the figure move slightly, her head tilting to one side. "We'll see. In time you'll realize it's the right thing to do."

The light went out, and all was silent.

Macy sat perfectly still, barely daring to breathe as she waited for her tormentor to move or say more. After several minutes, it was as if her twin had disappeared into thin air. She was unsure how long she sat there, her body stiff with fear. Her limbs ached, and her eyeballs felt like someone had coated them in grit by the time she finally relaxed enough to go back to sleep.

When she eventually dragged herself out of bed in the morning, her room was back to normal. The lamp was where it had always been on the nightstand. It was on and now unnecessary in the morning's light.

She rubbed her face. She had to rid herself of this hallucination before it completely pushed her over the edge. The dreams were beginning to feel too real.

With a stretch, she slipped her feet into her slippers and put on her robe. A yawn escaped as she shuffled down the stairs, through the foyer, and into the kitchen.

She wasn't fully awake until her foot connected with something and it went sliding across the tile floor.

Her eyes followed the piece of white ceramic, and she frowned. She crouched to inspect the remaining pieces of the object. It didn't take her long to realize she was looking at the remnants of her favorite coffee mug. The one her father had given her.

"What the hell?" She whispered as she picked up the bigger pieces.

Tears welled in her eyes as she stood and moved them to the counter. That mug was one of the few things that survived the fire unscathed. And now it was in too many pieces to repair a second time.

She grabbed the broom and swept up the slivers that were scattered on the tile.

She took a deep breath and then blew it out, repeating in a careful, controlled rhythm.

Her palm brushed away tears as she steadied herself to finish cleaning the mess.

"I will not cry over a mug." She said in a low tone. "I will not cry over a mug." She repeated the mantra a few more times as she swept, trying to convince herself it wasn't worth the tears.

She did not know how the mug broke, but she knew there was little use in making a scene over it, even if she was alone in her kitchen.

Once she'd cleared the mess, she started the coffeepot and grabbed another mug to use. The black mug with palm trees had been a gift from Troy on one of his assignments. She poured her coffee and sat at the table.

Macy turned in her chair and stared at the floor where the mess had been. That mug had been in her cabinet when she went to bed last night. She was sure of it.

Did she get up in the night and not remember? Nothing made sense anymore. Her coffee forgotten, she put her hands in her face and cried.

It was becoming too much. She wasn't sleeping, despite going back on the medications. Her hallucinations were threatening her, and in those moments she was struggling to determine what was real and what wasn't. Something had to give soon, and she was afraid it would be her sanity, if it wasn't already too late.

She allowed herself to cry it out. All the emotions she'd been bottling up since this ordeal began. She couldn't be strong right now. Macy just didn't have it in her. She needed support. She needed her uncle or Troy.

The sobs became more intense as her mind flashed back to when she was a little girl and all the times her father had held her and dried her tears. She needed her parents so desperately at that moment.

"Cry baby." The hiss of words seemed to come from everywhere and she jumped, causing her chair to scoot back. She slid out of it and on to the floor.

Without thinking, she crawled under the table and held on to one leg as if it were her only salvation.

Macy stayed as quiet as possible as she listened for any

sign she wasn't alone. Her tears drying to her face as she watched and waited.

"You can't escape me." The voice hissed again.

She closed her eyes and shook her head. "No. No. You will not win. I won't let you." Her voice became louder with each word. "I will not allow this! You hear me!" Macy was trying to fight back, despite the fact that her mind was the enemy here. "Go away! You aren't welcome here. You aren't welcome in my head!"

She put her hands over her ears, as if doing so could block out anything else her hallucination had to say to her.

Macy's phone rang, and she scrambled out from under the table to grab it. She almost dropped it in her haste to answer.

"Hello?" She knew her voice had to sound frantic, but she didn't care. She needed someone to ground her.

"Macy? Are you okay?" Troy's voice sent a frisson of clarity through her.

"Yes. I'm okay. I'm so glad you called." She sat herself back down at the table, then thought better of it and moved into the living room. She settled in on the sofa as he talked. She focused on his voice.

"You don't sound okay. You sound… upset. And like you might be losing your voice. Are you sick?" His concern for her was always so endearing.

"I'm okay now that you've called." She smiled. "Do you have plans for today?"

"I have to finish a few things at work, but it's not a full day. Do you want me to come over?"

She gave herself a moment to consider what she was about to say. Did she dare tell him about all that's happened? What if he left her? What if he decided she was too much to deal with?

It was a chance she had to take. She needed to talk to someone other than Dr. Yates.

"Yes, if you could, that'd be nice. I could use the company and I have something to tell you." Nerves caused her voice to waver a little, and she worked quickly to correct it.

"I don't like the sound of that." He whispered.

"No, it's not bad. Well, I mean, it's not bad about us. It's something else I'm dealing with. I need your support." She couldn't tell him over the phone. This was going to be difficult, and she needed to see his face when she told him she was losing her marbles. She had to witness his reaction.

"Okay, sure. I can be over around two. Would that work?"

Macy looked at her watch. "Yes, that's perfect."

"Okay, I'll see you then."

"See you then." She hung up the phone, only just then realizing that he'd not told her why he called. She'd have to remember to ask him when he arrived. Macy felt terrible that she'd only been focused on herself during that conversation.

She glanced at her watch. Only five hours to go. She could stay occupied until then. She'd paint or watch a movie. Anything to keep her mind from wandering to wherever it was her hallucinations had decided to live.

he doorbell rang at precisely two sharp and Macy skipped down the hall, happy to finally see Troy. The last several hours had seemed to stretch on forever. She was fine at first, painting for an hour and then having lunch. After she'd watched a movie, then spent the rest of the time sitting on the sofa, praying Troy would arrive soon.

She'd started to mentally replay the night before, and it

wasn't something she wanted to think about when she was alone.

She opened the door and Troy was standing on her doorstep, a bouquet of mixed flowers so large it completely obscured the upper half of his body.

She laughed. "What in the world?"

He stepped inside and lowered the vase. "It sounded like you were having a bad day, so I brought a Macy-needs-pampered kit with me."

She took the flowers and set them on a side table in the foyer. "That's so sweet of you."

He produced a brown paper grocery bag as well. "There's more." He pushed passed her and made his way to the kitchen. She pursued him after taking one last glance at the gorgeous floral arrangement now in her entryway.

When she stepped into the kitchen, he was unloading items on to her table.

"I bought chicken Alfredo we can heat for dinner, cookies and cream ice cream for dessert, and…" He put something behind his back and stepped closer to her. "You're favorite movie for a romantic night in." He pulled the DVD from behind his back and handed it to her.

"Sabrina!" She squealed with glee. He knew the way to her heart. She was so happy at his thoughtfulness, she'd almost forgotten why she'd wanted him to come over.

Troy pulled her close and kissed her forehead. "Only the best for my girl."

Macy smiled and released a contented sigh as she enjoyed the gentle caresses he administered up and down her back.

He stepped back and grabbed the ice cream. Troy turned to put it in the freezer when he saw the large pieces of the broken mug. "Oh no. What happened?"

Her eyes moved to the evidence still on the counter. "It's

a long story, and part of why I needed you to come over."

He nodded. "Okay. Whenever you're ready." He put the food away and then ushered her into the living room. "What do we do first, movie or talk?"

They sat together on the sofa, and she faced him. "We should probably talk. If you still want to watch the movie after, I'm more than fine with that."

He nodded, but she could see the alarm in his eyes.

"But first, tell me what you called about earlier."

He smiled. "Oh, it's great news. I got that feature from my boss. The one I'd been asking for."

She yelped in delight and hugged his neck. "That's so wonderful."

He kissed her. "It is. Now, what is it you have to tell me?"

She took a deep breath. "So… I've been seeing things." She spilled the beans on all the things she'd experienced so far.

He listened intently, nodding and seeming to understand. When she finished with the cup and the voice in the kitchen, he blew out a bewildered breath.

"Damn. That's some scary stuff to deal with all on your own." He took her hands in his. "Why didn't you tell me sooner?"

She shrugged. "I guess I worried you be done with me. Or you'd suggest I commit myself."

He pulled her to him, wrapping his arms around her tight. "Never. I told you before, I'm in this for the long haul."

She hugged him back as tears of relief fell. Macy had never had anyone, besides her uncle, that she could count on before. She wondered if she was falling in love with him. It was nice to have someone to lean on and care for, but it also terrified her. Something could rip people away from you so easily. And then you are left with nothing.

8

MACY

acy had gone more than a week without seeing her doppelgänger. She hoped and prayed that somehow, it was all over. She wanted to go back to how things were before her conscious had started visibly stalking her. Her previous episodes weren't always easy to deal with; flashbacks, voices from her past, faces full of terror, fears of shadows that were simply shadows, but she'd take those any day over her most recent aberrations.

She somewhat felt better. Not normal, as she hadn't known normal in over a decade. But she felt less foreboding with each day that passed without an "angry twin" sighting.

Her last visit with Dr. Yates had gone well. She'd told him about seeing her doppelgänger in her room and together they'd decided it was likely a nightmare or possibly sleep paralysis, although nightmare made more sense to her. She still didn't like it, but a nightmare was better than a hallu-cination.

She'd almost finished the commission for her uncle's friend, but had concerns about the product so far. It was a little darker than her previous pieces. She was sure her recent experiences had something to do with that, but she couldn't bring herself to paint anything else. It was what felt right, despite her struggles. Hopefully, the last little details would make it perfect and something Mrs. Chase would love.

Her cell phone rang just as she'd finished cleaning her brushes.

She placed her brushes in their drying rack and balanced the phone between her shoulder and ear. "Hello?"

"Hey, Macy. It's Jenn." Her voice was soft and a little sad.

"Hi Jenn. How are you? Is everything okay?"

Jenn cleared her throat. "I just wanted to apologize yet again. Please know that I'm really sorry about leaving you at the art supply store. I'm not sure where the miscommunication happened, but it wasn't intentional. I swear."

"No, please don't apologize. I told you to go get lunch. I'm the one that ran off." Macy moved the phone to her other ear and took a seat in the kitchen.

"Macy… that's not what you told me yesterday. You yelled at me, in front of my boss. I almost got fired." Anger laced Jenn's voice.

Macy frowned. "What? I didn't talk to you yesterday."

"You came to the restaurant and chewed me out in the dining room. In front of customers and my manager. You don't remember that?" Jenn huffed.

Macy shook her head. "No. That's impossible. I was here all day. I was working. The only way I could have gotten to your work was by calling you. You know how I am."

"I thought I did, but it was most definitely you, Macy McCall." Jenn sounded hurt. "And I don't think I've ever heard such mean things come out of your mouth." She sighed loudly. "Maybe it's time you go back to that doctor of yours and change your medications."

"Jenn, I swear. I don't remember any of that. I'm sure I

didn't leave the house." Macy felt the pressure rise in her chest.

Jenn reacted as if she didn't hear her. "But when you go back to that fancy doctor, be sure you call someone else to drive you. I'm done." Jenn hung up the phone.

Macy stood in place, the phone still up to her ear. *What just happened?* She was sure she hadn't left the house yesterday. She ran through the day in her mind.

Breakfast.

Coffee on the balcony while she meditated.

Painting for Mrs. Chase.

Lunch.

Nap.

Wait. What did she do after the nap? She remembered talking to Troy on the phone and having dinner, but she couldn't remember what happened between her nap, which was unusual in itself, and dinner.

Was it possible? How could she have made it anywhere without calling Jenn?

It made zero sense.

She grabbed her phone and called Troy.

"Hey sweetheart." His voice floated over the speaker like a breath of fresh air.

"Hey, I have a weird question." She reminded herself that this had to be a misunderstanding.

"Shoot." She heard him fidgeting with something and assumed he had one of his cameras in his hand.

"Did I have you take me anywhere yesterday? Like to the restaurant Jenn works at?" She felt stupid for having to ask.

"Nooooo." He drew the word out slowly. "Why?"

"Because Jenn just called me. She said I came to see her at work and yelled at her."

He scoffed. "You? Yelling at someone?"

She rolled her eyes. "That's not so much my point. She says I was there. How would I have gotten there without her picking me up? It had to be you or Uncle Robbie."

"You're saying you went but don't remember how you got there?" He asked.

"I'm saying I don't remember doing it at all. But there's only three ways I could have gotten there and two of them are now out." She blew out a frustrated breath. "I'm worried, Troy."

"Wow. I don't know, sweetheart." She heard another click.

"I'm sorry. I know you're working. I'll let you go. Just one more question. Did I mention going anywhere at all when we talked before dinner?" She tensed up, unsure what answer she really hoped to hear.

"No, not a word. We talked about the next movie we want to see, and when we'd plan another date once I get back from my new assignment." Another clicking sound.

"Okay. Well, I'll let you go. Have a safe trip. Take pretty pictures. Make lots of money." She forced a smile, hoping it would transfer through her words and make her sound way less worried than she actually was.

"You sure you're okay?" He wasn't buying it.

"Yes, I'm sure. I'll call my uncle. I'm sure he can help me figure it out."

"If you're sure." He repeated.

"I am. Talk to you soon." She smiled for real this time.

"I'll call you when I get there. Later, sweetheart."

The line went dead.

Macy's thoughts were racing as fast as her heartbeat. Uncle Robbie was her last grasp at an explanation, yet she knew what his answer would be. She wanted to believe she could trust herself enough to know if she'd left the house or not, but as before she couldn't account for her time in the afternoon of question.

She dialed her uncle as tears formed in her eyes.

"Robbie McCall speaking."

"Hey, Uncle Robbie. Listen, I could use some company. Could you come over for dinner tonight?"

*U*ncle Robbie sat at the table and smiled at her. "This is nice."

She returned his smile. "Yes, it is. It's been a little too long since we just had a simple dinner and conversation."

He nodded as he loaded a last bite of steak onto his fork. "It's been far too long since I've had your cooking." He patted his stomach. "I was wasting away."

She laughed and looked at his somewhat rotund figure. "Yes, I'm surprised you haven't blown away in the wind by now."

He chewed, pointing a fork at her. Once he swallowed he replied with "I don't need sass from you, little miss."

She smirked as she sipped her wine.

"So," he placed his fork on the plate. "What happened?"

Her eyebrows rose in unison. "Happened?"

He narrowed his eyes, his lips pressed into a thin line. "Don't act like you have no clue what I mean. Something happened or you wouldn't have asked me over."

She picked up her plate, then his. "Done?"

He nodded.

She walked into the kitchen, and he followed. "Don't avoid the question."

She started loading the dishwasher. "I may or may not be having blackouts where I lose time."

"You what?" Alarm laced his words.

"I know. It's weird." She said as she placed a baking dish on the rack.

"Weird? Weird doesn't cover it. What does Dr. Yates think?" He put a hand on her arm to stop her from over scrubbing a cup.

"We haven't discussed it yet. It's sort of new. I'll have to bring it up Monday." She placed the cup in the sink.

"Do you need me to stay with you until then? I can probably rearrange part of my schedule."

"No. Absolutely not." She turned to face him fully. "I just need you to know about it. And ask you..." she sighed. "I need to ask you if I had you take me anywhere yesterday."

He shook his head. "Is that one of your lost moments?"

She nodded. She didn't want to worry him, but she had to ask to be sure. "I somehow made it down to Jenn's work and I guess yelled at her. Got her in trouble with her boss. She won't be driving me anymore."

He frowned. "That doesn't sound like you."

She shrugged. "I know, but she swears I did it."

"Odd." He scrunched up his face as he mulled that information over.

Macy dried her hands and placed the dish towel on the counter. "I'm going to go take my meds. Mrs. Chase's painting is in my studio if you want to check it out. I'll be right back."

"Wonderful." He turned his back and walked opposite the direction she was heading.

She bounced up the stairs, feeling some joy at having her uncle there, even though it was only for another hour or so.

She entered her bedroom and decided she'd get more comfortable as well. She quickly changed into sweatpants and a baggy t-shirt, then stepped into the bathroom where she took her evening pill. As she walked past one of the empty bedrooms near hers, the hairs on the back of her neck stood on end.

She froze in the hallway. The door to that room was partially open, and she thought she heard someone inside.

"Uncle Robbie?" She called out, much softer than she'd intended.

She stepped backwards slowly, inching closer to the door.

Someone was moving in there, but the lights were off. She never turned off the lights. Every room had at least one lamp on. It was part of her comforting process.

With just two more steps, she was even with the doorway. In the center of the room, just at the edge of the bed, a figure stood, partially in shadow. Dark hair cascaded down the intruder's back. She wore sweats and a t-shirt.

Macy couldn't move. She couldn't breathe. She couldn't function.

The figure turned and looked at her. "It's always fun to look at family photos, don't you think?" The voice whispered harshly.

Macy's eyes darted to the bed. She could see small sections of the area thanks to the light filtering in behind her from the hall. Dozens of scattered photos covered the surface of the comforter.

Macy's double stepped a little closer where the light gave her features more definition.

Yet again the resemblance floored Macy.

"What are you doing?" Macy whispered.

"I'm enjoying all the memories of our childhood." She smiled, but there was no joy in the gesture. "We were a lucky girl, were we not? Daddy loved us so much. Mother doted on us with all the pretty things." She looked at the bed once more. "So many photos to prove how much they loved us."

Macy wanted to scream for her uncle, but no sound would escape. Her voice had abandoned her.

Macy's double stepped even closer. "You ruined it all. You let everyone down. But then, is that really a surprise? You always were a selfish little bitch."

"Don't you mean us?" Macy squeaked out.

"No, not with that. Selfishness was always your problem."

Macy realized her vocal chords were once more cooperating. She screamed. "Uncle Robbie! Come quickly!" She kept her eyes trained on her double.

The double laughed. "Good luck trying to prove I exist. No one can see me but you." She stepped backward until the shadows swallowed her once more.

Macy wanted to run in after her, but her feet wouldn't move. They glued her to the spot.

Robbie took the steps two at a time. "What's wrong?" His eyes frantically searched the hall.

"I…" how did she explain this? She still hadn't mentioned her doppelgänger. She feared he'd think she'd need to be hospitalized. "Could you turn on that light for me?"

She knew it was cowardly, but she couldn't make herself enter the room.

He gave her a funny look, nodded, and stepped inside. In moments, light filled the room, illuminating every corner.

Macy stepped across the threshold tentatively. Only her uncle occupied the room.

He looked at the photos on the bed. "Where did you get all these photos?" He picked them up and inspected each one. A look of alarm crossed his face as he looked at one photo, then back at Macy.

"What?" She asked, leaning forward.

"Nothing, really. I just hadn't seen some of these in a while. Would you mind if I took them with me? I wouldn't mind reminiscing a little." He smiled at her. "I miss them so much."

She sure as hell didn't want them, and she didn't even know what they were, other than family photos. She couldn't imagine looking at a single one without seeing her double's sneering face. Especially since she didn't understand how they got there. "Yes, please feel free."

He quickly gathered them up and tucked them under his arm. "I'll bring them back, I promise."

She tried to act nonchalant. "No hurry. I've seen them all." *Liar*, her brain screamed.

He nodded. "Thank you. I appreciate it."

He shuffled past her and down the stairs. Macy cautiously stepped into the center of the room where her hallucination had just been. Her eyes roamed the room, but she was now totally alone. She wasn't sure if that comforted her or scared her. Her mind didn't seem to be her own anymore. And that was a reality she wasn't ready to accept.

She stepped out of the room, giving it a last look before heading back downstairs.

She would have had to put the photos there. A hallucination couldn't do that. Yet she not only had zero recollection of doing so, but she was quite sure she'd never seen those particular photos before. The few she got a good look at resembled nothing she had in her family album. There weren't that many salvaged from the fire. How did she end up with them?

She worried this vision of herself had a lot of secrets. She'd have to discuss this with Dr. Yates for sure. Maybe she was developing another personality, or this was some strange alternative way of coping. Was her brain finding fresh ways to deal with the truths that were coming out in therapy?

She couldn't recall any big revelations since seeing Dr. Yates, but he had a way of helping her express her concerns, and he encouraged her to acknowledge the emotions she felt during her worst moments. He also allowed her to relive memories, and sometimes those were hazy and seemed out of sync with the timelines she remembered. *Has she always had a double? Another version of herself, full of anger and disgust?* She wished she knew. But so little seemed clear anymore. Maybe one day she'd actually have all the answers. Today she'd have to settle for the fact that she wasn't well, and the people that loved her were there to help.

9

TROY

Troy put the last of his photography gear in his rental car and shut the door. His latest assignment had been a challenge, but he was excited about the opportunity. It wasn't everyday his boss offered him the main photo essay in their magazine. He loved freelancing, but being an employee of Carefree Travel Magazine wasn't anything to thumb his nose at. It was a small publication, but it was steady work that paid relatively well. This particular spread was going to help put his name on the map. Thanks to the magazine owner having a close friendship with a filthy rich tech mogul, he'd just finished photographing the most exclusive and private island home in existence.

Granted, no one could visit there, so it wasn't a travel article, but it showed what kind of beautiful places were out there if you searched hard enough. He photographed the owner and the home in a way to showcase the stress-free life that island living can offer. Having a shit-ton of money certainly didn't hurt either, but he minimized that point as much as possible. This was partly to stroke the ego of the billionaire and partly to make his life seem achievable, even if only for a weekend.

Troy had just reached the airport when his cell phone rang.

He saw Macy's name on the caller ID and smiled. "Hey, sweetheart!"

"Hi, Troy." Her voice was soft.

"Is everything okay?" He couldn't help the fission of alarm that shot through him. She sounded off.

"Yeah, everything is fine. I just miss you." Her tone stayed quiet.

"I miss you too, baby. I'll be back home tonight. I know we weren't supposed to get together until tomorrow night, but do you want me to come by?" He smiled at the thought of seeing her.

"How about I come see you?" There was a hint of uncertainty in her words.

"Are you sure? You've only been to my apartment one time. I mean, I don't mind at all, I just want to be sure you're comfortable with it." He popped the trunk, and a skycap took his bags.

"I'm sure. You've already done so much traveling recently. No reason I can't make the quick trip to see you."

He handed his flight info to the skycap and switched the phone to his other hand. "If you're sure. You'll have your uncle bring you, then?"

"Ah, no. But I'll get a cab." He thought he heard a bit more excitement in her voice this time, and it made him smile wider.

"A cab? A regular cab?" He was even more surprised by this suggestion than by her coming over.

"Sure, why not? I need to get adventurous and wild sometime. I'll start with a cab."

He chuckled. "Wow. I guess so. Looking forward to it. I gotta run and catch my flight, babe." He walked to the car rental counter as he talked.

She chuckled. "See? I'm making progress. I'll see you soon." She paused and took a deep breath. "Troy?"

"Yes?"

"I think… I think I'm in love with you." She pushed the words out in one hurried breath.

He stopped in his tracks. "You love me?"

"Yes." She breathed.

He chuckled. "I know I love you, Macy. I think I have from the first date."

She released a nervous laugh. "I'll see you tonight."

"See you then." He put the phone in his pocket and allowed himself to stand in the middle of the airport while he grinned like an idiot. They hadn't said 'I love you' yet. He didn't think the first time would be over the phone, but he'd take it. He'd take whatever he could get from her, because damn it all, he was head over heels for Macy McCall.

He'd been home about an hour when Macy arrived at his apartment. Troy opened the door and almost dropped his beer. He'd always thought her beautiful. She was the kind of girl that preferred minimal makeup and baggy clothes. She didn't like to fuss over her looks, and honestly, he didn't care if she wore a potato sack. He thought she was one of the loveliest women he'd ever known. But standing before him was a goddess. She'd curled her hair and pulled it back in a loose bun. Several small tendrils fell, teasing the delicate skin around her neck.

Her make up looked like something from a glamour

magazine, it accentuated her features, but wasn't excessive. She practically glowed.

He stepped aside, and she entered, taking off her coat. Again, words failed him. She dropped her coat over the back of his sofa and turned to face him.

"Do you like it?" She smiled coyly.

He could only nod as his eyes roamed the curves she'd never allowed him, or possibly anyone else, to see before. He cleared his throat. "What… uh… when did you get that dress?"

She looked down at the clothing in question. The form-fitting red spandex perfectly matched the red of her new lipstick. The neckline gave him an excellent view of her cleavage and the length of the skirt didn't reach her knees.

"I finally went shopping for something pretty. I thought it was time to stop hiding behind my hobo clothing." She smiled as she showed him one tantalizing leg. "I even bought matching heels."

He nodded in appreciation. "I like it very much."

"I'm glad." She turned and walked farther into his living area. "Can I get a drink?"

It took him a moment to shake himself from his stupor. "Oh yeah, sure. What would you like?"

"What are you having?" She peered at the can in his hand.

"Just a beer. Keeping it simple tonight. Long day." He grinned at her.

"I'll have one."

His brows knit together. "I thought you didn't like beer."

She shrugged. "I'm trying to break out of my safe little mold. Maybe if I try it again, I'll like it." She put a hand on her hip. "Dr. Yates says I gotta step out of my comfort zone now and then, so… here I am."

"Huh," Troy mulled that over a second. "Makes sense."

He suddenly worried her confession of love earlier in the day was just her trying something. Surely she wouldn't test the waters with something so serious, would she?

He walked to the fridge and got her a beer, opening it for her so she wouldn't damage her fresh manicure.

"Thank you." She took a dainty sip. "Not as bad as last time. I think I could get used to it."

He held his can up. "To trying new things."

She smiled and held hers up as well. "Absolutely. To trying new things."

They both took a drink, and she sat her beer on a nearby table. Macy stepped close to him and wrapped her arms around his neck.

"Macy," Troy began. "I have to admit, I'm a little surprised by all this. We've moved very slow to give you time to adjust to everything."

Her fingers traced tiny circles on the back of his neck, her touch increasing his need to touch her back. "I think on some things, we've been going a little too slow, Troy." She leaned into him and kissed him lightly on the lips.

His hands, which had been lightly resting on her hips, were now moving to her back. She deepened the kiss, and he moaned, unable to break from the desire she was building within him.

In a moment of clarity, he pushed her away. "Sweetheart, we can't keep that up. I'm not going to be able to take much more."

She captured her bottom lip between her teeth and looked into his eyes. "What am I doing to you, Troy?"

He shook his head. "You're driving me crazy." He took a step back to put some space between them. "I'm not saying this is the first time I've wanted you. There have been plenty of other times I've come home with a case of blue balls, but… wow. There is just something different tonight.”

“Different?” Her big brown eyes looked up at him with such an innocence that he almost believed she was oblivious to her effect on him.

“You’re always sexy, Macy, but tonight… I’m afraid if we start anything I’ll have a hard time stopping. I don’t want to put that kind of pressure on you. I love you too much to do anything that might risk our relationship.” He ran a hand through his hair. “I can wait until you’re ready.”

She reached for him, but he didn’t move, so she stepped closer once more and took his hand. “Troy, what if I am ready? Now.”

He searched her face. She’d never been a tease. He’d understood that while she loved being with him and being close, it was difficult for her to allow him certain intimacies. She struggled to get close to people. Could she really have overcome that so soon? He thought it’d take a lot longer.

“Why now?” He asked.

She seemed to weigh her words carefully. “I think because I realized that life is short, and some things aren’t going to wait on me to get better. I don’t want to miss out on the good things because I’m scared of some bad things.” She sighed. “And because I love you. And I trust you.”

He smiled and ran the back of his fingers down her cheek. “I love you so much, Macy.”

She placed her hand over his and pressed her cheek into his palm. She closed her eyes. “I love you too, Troy. I’m sorry it’s taken me this long to say it.”

He shook his head. “I don’t care how long it took, as long as it’s true.” He leaned forward and kissed her again. She once again deepened the kiss, and this time he didn’t hesitate to follow her lead.

She pulled back and lead him to the sofa, pushing him down to a seated position. He couldn't tear his eyes from her as she reached back and unzipped the dress, letting it fall to her feet. He reached for her and she moved to him, straddling him as she kissed him with a ferocity he didn't know she possessed.

He allowed his hands to roam her back, and that's when he felt the scars. He stopped.

She froze as well and pulled away to look into his face. "Do they bother you?"

He shook his head. "No, I just didn't expect them. I knew you'd been injured but I didn't know it'd been so extensive."

"Some places are bad." She dropped her eyes and he could feel her self-consciousness creeping back in.

He put his hands on either side of her face, forcing her to look at him. "Don't be ashamed of them. Ever. Those are battle scars that prove you survived. That you are a fighter and you are still here."

She nodded, a tear rolling down her cheek. He picked her up and carried her to his bed. Once he'd placed her on her stomach where he could get better access to her back, he slowly took his time kissing each raised, angry welt that she hated, hoping to prove to her once and for all that she never had to hide any part of herself from him.

He spent the rest of the night showing her just how much he loved her; scars, complications, and all.

⁜

The next morning Troy awoke to an empty bed. He sat up and looked around. He saw no trace of Macy's things.

He swung his feet over the side of the bed and stretched. *Did last night really happen?*

His feet hit the floor and before putting his full weight on them, he felt something sharp stab his heel.

"Shit!" He pulled his foot up quickly. Sticking out from his skin was one of the diamond studs Macy had worn the night before.

He removed it, then took it to the bathroom to wash it off. He'd be sure to take it to her when he saw her later. Troy hated that she'd snuck out on him, but maybe, in the light of morning, she'd become overwhelmed by last night's activities. It wasn't uncommon for her to experience anxiety after trying something out of her comfort zone. Last night was without a doubt out of the norm for her. But he was proud of her.

He'd be lying if he said he didn't enjoy the sex. They'd been dating for months with no real physical intimacy, and he was doing his best to assure she was comfortable with any steps they took. But last night was like something out of his fantasies. His pride in her moved beyond that. He was proud that she'd faced something that previously scared her. It wasn't just about the physical for her, it was also emotional and mental. She feared letting others get too close. She'd said as much after their first few dates. Almost everyone she'd ever loved had been lost in one horrible night. It scarred her in every way that trauma can leave a mark on a person.

Macy allowing him into the house recently had encouraged him quite a bit. Maybe she was finally trusting him with her heart. He hoped so. Because he fully intended to spend the rest of his life making sure Macy McCall knew she was loved and cared for as she deserved.

10

MACY

The doorbell rang, and Macy jumped in her seat. She glanced at her watch. "Shit, is it five already?"

She put down her brush and wiped a smear of paint on her smock. "Coming!"

As she approached the door, she heard Troy's voice. "Hey, it's me."

Once the door was unlocked, she cracked the door to assure it was Troy. She could no longer trust what she saw and heard, so her extra caution felt warranted. He smiled at her from the doorway, his hands behind his back.

"Hey, so sorry. I lost track of time while painting." She swung the door open wide so he could enter.

He produced a bouquet of red roses. He was always so sweet about getting her flowers. "It's okay. We get there when we get there."

Macy smiled and accepted the flowers. "They're beautiful."

Troy stepped inside and she moved to lock the door. "No, let me. You go get those in some water."

She nodded. "Oh, um… Okay, thank you."

It was hard for her to allow someone else the responsibility of her safety. She needed to assure the locks on all doors were secure. Not that she expected him to ignore the task or preform it incorrectly, she just needed to know it was done. It was another aspect of her paranoia.

"I'll be right back." She hurried down the hall to the kitchen and grabbed a large crystal vase from the cabinet. In minutes, she had water and roses artfully arranged in the vase.

When she entered the living room, she found Troy standing near the fireplace, looking at the family photos arranged on the mantel.

"That one is my mother." She said softly.

He smiled. "You look just like her."

Macy smiled at the remark. "Yeah, I do. I hope to someday be the kind of woman she was."

Troy raised his eyebrows in question.

"Mom was always helping the less fortunate or volunteering for various causes. She put herself out there for people."

He nodded. "She sounds like an amazing woman."

"She was." Macy cleared her throat of the emotion that threatened to choke her.

"You're an amazing woman too." He stepped closer and put his arms around her. "You're kind, generous, and creative. Just because you can't physically be present doesn't mean you aren't helping as much as she did. You just do it through donations and your talent."

She put her forehead to his chest. "You think so?"

He placed a finger under her chin and lifted her face so she could look into his eyes. "I know so."

Troy leaned in to kiss her lips. It was soft and sweet at

first, then he deepened it and his grip on her became a little more passionate.

Macy pushed him away. "I'm sorry. I just…"

He dropped his hands to his sides. "No, I'm sorry. I'm so happy that we are finally getting close, but I should assume nothing about us until we've talked about it."

She gave him a small smile. "Yes, thank you. I'm glad we are getting close too." She glanced at the staircase. "I guess I should go get ready for dinner."

He put his hands behind him. "Yes, I should let you do that." He cleared his throat. "What other new clothes did you get? After that red dress, I'm dying to see what other surprises you have."

She turned to face him fully. "Red dress?"

"The one you wore last night." He added.

"Last night?" She knew she sounded like an idiot, but she was completely lost.

He frowned. "You don't remember last night?"

She shook her head slowly.

"Oh, no." He blew out a breath that reminded her of her uncle when he was unsure what to say next.

"What the fuck happened last night?" She rarely cursed around him, but was afraid of the answer. Her language always got coarse when fear took over.

He blinked rapidly. "You came over. And we… well, we took an additional step in our relationship." His expression looked as if he worried she'd break. He pulled something from his pocket. "I almost forgot. You left this at my apartment. I stepped on it this morning, but I don't think I bent the post." He put the diamond stud in her palm.

Macy stared at it. "I don't understand."

Troy sat on the sofa and put his head in his hands. "I don't know how to explain this."

"This isn't mine, Troy. And I don't own a fucking red dress." She felt her heart pick up its pace. Could she have possibly had another episode where she'd done something she didn't remember? Like with Jenn?

"Macy, I don't know how to convince you, but you were there, with me, last night."

She waved him to follow her. "I'll show you."

Macy assumed he'd follow as she didn't have the courage to turn and face him just then. She heard his footsteps behind hers on the stairs and braced herself for whatever might come next. She was no longer sure what to expect.

She pushed open her bedroom door and walked to the large walk-in closet. She flipped the switch and the small room filled with light.

"See? I have blue, gray, black… even some white. No red in my closet." She leaned in the doorway but kept her eyes on the floor. "I look awful in red."

Troy pushed passed her and moved to the rack near the back. "No, you don't. And I'm talking about this one."

She looked up to see him holding a slinky red dress. One she'd never seen before.

"What?" She stumbled backward and stopped when she hit her bed frame.

Troy walked out of the closet, dress in hand. "This is what you wore last night."

Tears filled her eyes. "Troy, I honest to God don't remember buying that dress, let alone wearing it."

She stood and moved to her dresser, opening a small box on top. She rummaged through until she found what she'd been looking for. A small card held her favorite pair of diamond studs. One was missing.

Tears rolled down her cheeks. "Oh, shit. What is happening to me?"

Troy stepped next to her and placed the earring on the dresser. "I don't know, but we'll figure it out." He kissed the side of her head.

She turned to face him. "Did we..." she couldn't finish the question.

"Did we have sex?" He looked into her eyes.

She nodded.

"Yes, we did." He smiled. "But we don't have to again. Not until we know you are ready."

She released a humorless laugh. "Our first time together and I don't even remember it. Figures."

He frowned. "I'm so sorry, Macy."

She shook her head. "If I instigated things, you have nothing to be sorry for."

He sighed. "I know."

"Well?" She joked. "Was it good?" She decided she need to laugh before she broke down completely.

"It was amazing." The look on his face reflected the joy in his words.

Now she really hated that she didn't remember it. She shrugged, trying to keep the conversation light and fun. "I can't exactly argue the point."

His jaw dropped as if offended. "Miss McCall, I'm shocked. How dare you suggest I could be lying?"

Macy chuckled. "I didn't say that. But you have to admit, you weren't going to say it was awful."

He straightened his collar. "Of course not. I'm not a fucking idiot." He winked at her and she relaxed a little. Troy just cursed in front of her. He'd always told her that proper gentlemen didn't use vulgar language in front of ladies. It's why she'd been so determined to watch her own mouth around him. But now she felt he was showing her, in his own way, that he was with her. She didn't know what the hell was going on with her the last few days, but at least Troy was still on her side.

Macy sat in Dr. Yates' office, her head in her hands.

"It was so humiliating, Dr. Yates." She groaned and sat back in the chair like a defeated child.

Daniel frowned. "So you've had two episodes where you did something you don't remember doing?"

She nodded. "Yes. And both were horrible things." She sighed. "Well, one was horrible. Yelling at Jenn was unforgivable. Having sex with Troy was wonderful, according to him. I sadly can't remember it." She bolted upright. "What if I do that to a stranger?"

Daniel leaned forward. "You mean have sex with a stranger?"

She put her hands over her eyes. "Oh God. Can I even be trusted to take care of myself at this point?"

"Macy," Daniel began. "You have connections with Jenn and Troy. Your subconscious may have blamed Jenn for not being there when you fell apart. You may have wanted to take that step with Troy, but didn't acknowledge it yet. These are connections you aren't as likely to make with strangers." He paused. "That being said, I am a little concerned that you don't have any memories of these events."

"Is it like sleepwalking?" She asked.

"I guess you could say that." He tapped his pen on his leg. "It's like a part of you fell asleep while another part of you took over."

She groaned. "Kill me now."

Daniel shook his head. "I know it's scary. We'll figure

this out. Do you recall anything specific happening before these lapses in time? Maybe a trigger or if you felt off?"

She shook her head. "Not that I can think of. Although…" Macy chewed her bottom lip as she thought about it. "I took naps both days. I was unusually tired for some reason. Just completely exhausted."

He nodded. "Okay, that's a place to start."

Macy sighed. "Yeah, that's all I remember. Going to sleep."

"Are you waking up in the same place you go to sleep?"

She frowned. "Yeah, I did. Both times."

He reached for a pad of paper on a side table and scribbled. "I'm going to call your general practitioner. I'll suggest an MRI to be sure there isn't something else going on. I don't want to alarm you, but these blackout sessions you're having aren't a normal part of PTSD. At least, the recorded instances of it are very rare."

"You think I have a tumor or something?" She felt an odd relief at the thought. At least that would be an explanation.

"I'm not sure. It'd just be good to see what's going on with your physical health. We need to assure we aren't missing something." He smiled, and she knew he was trying to reassure her it was just something routine.

It didn't feel routine.

"I have to go inside the machine?" Just the thought made her light-headed.

"You do, but they can give you something to relax you." He made more notes on the paper. "I'll talk to them about your current meds and we'll see what they can do to make the process as painless as possible."

She nodded. "I appreciate that."

She took a moment to compose her thoughts. "Do you

think I could be developing an alternative personality? Like dissociative identity disorder or schizophrenia?"

He smiled at her. "You've been looking up symptoms on the internet again?"

Her smile was slight, and she felt her cheeks heat. "A little."

He sighed. "Like the blackouts, it's not completely impossible. But let's make sure we have all the facts before we look at a new diagnosis." He leaned forward in his chair. "Macy, we want to be sure that you get the best possible care, no matter the circumstances. But do your best not to get panicked or worked up over anything until we've looked into some things, okay?"

She nodded. "Yes. I will stay level-headed and cool. Because that's what I'm known for."

He laughed. "Very good. I'm glad you're using your humor again. That will help you get through the tough moments."

"So laughter really is the best medicine?" She teased.

"It sure doesn't hurt." He smiled back at her.

She thought about that. It was laugh or cry. Or lose her shit. She'd rather laugh if she had to choose.

TROY

Troy and Macy entered the hospital, her hand squeezing his in a vice-like grip. He could tell this terrified her. The situation was less than ideal for her, for many reasons. He wasn't sure what terrified her more, the results of the test or the test itself.

No one wants to hear they have a tumor or some physical anomaly causing their brain to malfunction. On the other hand, he couldn't think of anyone that would enjoy hearing it's literally all in their head, either.

Dr. Yates was waiting for them at radiology. "I was here visiting a friend and saw you enter the building. Glad you are getting this checked out."

Macy blew out a nervous breath. "I appreciate you taking care of me."

Troy nodded in agreement. "Yes, thank you for looking out for her."

Dr. Yates smiled. "It's my pleasure. Hopefully, we'll get to the bottom of these blackouts."

A nurse handed her a clipboard. "It's important that you

fill this out completely. We especially need to know about any metal implants you may have."

Macy accepted the paperwork and took a seat, quickly setting to work on the questions.

Troy pulled Dr. Yates aside. "Do you think the scan will find anything?"

Dr. Yates shrugged. "It's hard to say."

Troy cleared his throat, his next words seeming to stick there. "What if you don't? What does that mean?"

Dr. Yates pressed his lips in a tight line. "It could be a few things, but those are things that Macy will have to discuss with you when she's ready."

Troy sighed. "I know you can't give me specifics, but… if they find nothing, is she going to be okay? If it's something like a split personality or… I don't know. Whatever causes stuff like that, can it be treated?"

Dr. Yates placed a hand on Troy's shoulder. "It can all be treated. Cured completely? I don't know, but all disorders have treatments. The medieval stigma that used to surround mental illness has thankfully lessened in recent years. We have a better idea how to treat disorders and we can help people live productive lives."

Troy smiled. "I'm glad to hear that." He turned to look at her. "She's already been through so much. Hopefully, whatever this is, it's simple to fix."

Dr. Yates nodded. "I hope so too."

A technician approached Macy and took her paperwork. "Are you ready, Macy?"

She nodded and shot a sidelong glance at Troy. He gave her a reassuring smile. "I'll be right here when you get out."

As they walked away, he could hear the nurse giving Macy instructions about what they'd give her to wear and what to expect.

They had planned on light sedation, so he hoped she was completely comfortable before going in.

Dr. Yates settled in on a large sofa in the waiting room, and Troy decided he needed some coffee. "I'm going to find a coffee pot, want anything?"

Dr. Yates smiled. "Coffee would be great, actually. Thanks. I believe they have some available in the cafeteria downstairs."

Troy looked at the doors Macy had disappeared through.

"She'll be fine, Troy. I'll find you if anything happens while you're getting coffee, but I expect she'll be in and out without incident."

He relaxed his shoulders. "Yeah, you're right. I'll be back in a few."

Troy walked down the hall, taking a couple of turns before finding the elevators. He entered and pushed the button to the basement floor. Once there, he quickly found the cafeteria and picked up a couple of coffees. Since he didn't know if the doctor liked his plain, he grabbed some creamer and sugar packets and made his way back to the elevators. An elderly couple had just entered, and he followed them inside. As the doors began to close, he looked up and almost dropped his coffees.

Macy stood in the hall, looking at him. She gave him a quick glance, then quickly walked away.

When had she come down here? Shouldn't she be upstairs starting her tests?

When he made it back to the waiting area, he handed the extra coffee to Dr. Yates.

"I know I've not been gone long, but what happened?" He sipped his drink.

Dr. Yates expression was puzzled. "What do you mean?"

"I could have sworn I just saw Macy down by the cafeteria." Troy said as he sat next to the doctor.

Dr. Yates sat down his coffee. "That's impossible. I've been here the entire time. She's not come out of imaging yet. She should be just getting started, actually."

Troy frowned. "I know, that's why it startled me. This girl looked a lot like her."

Dr. Yates sat quiet a moment, staring into his cup. "You think it was just someone who resembled her?"

"Well, yeah," said Troy. "Who else could it be?"

Dr. Yates nodded. "Yeah, you're right." He looked concerned though.

Troy shook his head. "I've not slept a lot lately. I think I'm just sleep deprived." He chuckled and took a sip fo his coffee.

Dr. Yates nodded. "Sleep deprivations will certainly mess with you."

They dropped the subject then and both men sat quietly as they waited for Macy to return. Troy flipped through magazines, occasionally stealing a glance at Dr. Yates. The doctor spent most of his time on his phone.

A nursing friend of Dr. Yates came through the doors, looked around, and spotted him. "Ah, Daniel." She gave him a pat on the back, then saw Troy. "Are you Macy's boyfriend?"

He nodded.

"Well, you'll both be happy to know that despite some minor anxiety, she's resting comfortably and they are beginning testing."

"Marla," Dr. Yates replied. "Has Miss McCall been in there the entire time since being taken back?"

Marla shot him an odd look. "Uh, yes. Why?"

Troy couldn't help himself. "By any chance did she go

down to the cafeteria a few minutes ago before starting her tests?"

Marla chuckled. "No, not at all." She looked at the two men. "What is going on? Why are you asking?"

They both shrugged it off.

"It's nothing, Marla." Replied Dr. Yates. "Thanks so much for the update."

She nodded and turned to go back inside when Troy stopped her. "Ma'am? Could you please tell Macy that I love her?"

She smiled brightly. "I will absolutely do that." The door swung wide as she pushed it open, and it shut with a loud click behind her.

Both men sat quietly for the rest of the wait. Troy spent his time wondering what he'd actually seen.

Macy stepped into the waiting room, with a hand on the arm of Marla.

Marla passed her off to Troy's care. "She's a little unsteady. The test can sometimes give you a bit of vertigo, but she should feel back to normal soon."

"Thank you." Troy replied as he put an arm around Macy.

Macy looked up into his face. "It's official. There is a brain."

Dr. Yates chuckled. "Well, that solves that mystery then."

Troy smiled, but his worry for her overshadowed the joke. He hoped that they'd have some actual answers soon.

He led Macy to his car and got her situated in the passenger seat.

"Ready to go home?" He asked.

She smiled at him, her eyes heavy lidded. "I think I'm still a little sedated. This is the calmest I've felt in years."

He chuckled. "So are you saying this is a good thing?"

She shrugged. "I'm not complaining, man."

He pulled away from the hospital and turned the car in the direction of her house. She snuggled into her seat and fell asleep.

He allowed her to rest until he pulled into her driveway.

"Sweetheart, we're home." He placed a hand on her arm.

She blinked slowly before opening her eyes. "Oh, good."

She sat up and stretched her legs out. "Are you coming in?"

Troy put a hand over hers. "I took the entire day off, just for you."

She leaned across the car and kissed him. "You're the bestest boyfriend ever."

He chuckled. "You're the doped-up girlfriend of my dreams."

She waved her hand at him. "You're just saying that because it's true."

He kissed her forehead, then got out of the car and jogged around to her side. He opened her door, and she climbed out, still a little unsteady on her feet.

"Allow me." He picked her up and carried her to the porch.

She giggled with delight.

"You are so loopy." He laughed and sat her down.

"I am." She unlocked the door and giggled.

They entered, and he locked up behind them. "What do we do now?"

"Good question. How does homemade panini and salad sound?" She walked toward the kitchen. "I think some food would wake me up."

He looked at his watch. "It's not technically lunchtime, but I am hungry. I vote yes."

She pulled various items out of the fridge. "I have ham and turkey. Preference? Both?"

She turned to get his answer and dropped a pitcher of lemonade. The pitcher shattered and sprinkled glass fragments all over the tile.

Troy jumped back, doing his best to avoid being hit by sharp projectiles. "Macy, what's wrong?"

She stared at him, but said nothing.

"Macy? Honey?" He carefully moved closer, avoiding the lemonade and glass on the floor.

It took him a moment to realize she wasn't staring at him, but past him. Her focus locked on something behind him. He turned and looked out the window into the backyard.

His blood ran cold. The garden shed door was open, with an unobstructed view inside.

"Macy, is that what I think it is?" He looked at her.

She shook her head. "I don't know how that got there."

He reached for her hand and helped her navigate the mess on the floor without injuring herself.

Once he assured she was safe, he stepped out the back door and crossed the yard.

Troy's steps slowed as he approached the shed.

"Holy shit." He muttered.

With careful steps, he moved forward, reaching for the light switch in the small building. He needed better light to confirm what he'd seen from in the house.

He sighed and looked over the mannequin hanging from a noose. Someone had taped Macy's photo to the face, her eyes scratched out.

He looked back at the house and didn't see her in the window.

He took a quick photo of it and considered taking it down, but then thought better of it. Maybe they should call the police. This certainly seemed like a threat, although part of him worried that this was another bit of mischief from her blackouts. If it turns out she'd done it, do they report it?

He knew she needed to make this call. It wasn't his decision to make.

He walked back to the house and found her waiting at the door.

"Is it what it looked like?" She asked timidly.

He nodded. "What do you want to do? I can take it down, or we can call the police."

She shook her head, and he thought he caught a tear before she quickly hid her face. He heard her take some deep breaths, then she raised her head and stared at the shed.

"Take it down. Please." Her voice held more conviction this time.

He thought they should call the police, but he suspected she was embarrassed enough. The same thing must have crossed her mind that had crossed his… she'd done this without knowing it.

1 2

———

MACY

$\mathcal{M}$acy had only a few minor touches left for Mrs. Chase's painting. It was without a doubt the darkest thing she'd ever painted. While it wasn't obviously violent or graphic, there was an undertone to it that made an astute viewer feel the terror and sadness in the strokes.

She sighed as she passed her art room. She didn't really have the energy to finish it today. But she'd be sure she'd complete it in time for Mrs. Chase's fundraising party the next week.

The doorbell rang and she rushed to answer it. She'd been waiting for Uncle Robbie's visit all day. She needed someone rational to keep her feeling sane.

As he entered, he landed a light peck on her cheek. "Hello, ladybug."

Macy locked up and followed him into the living room.

"How are you today?" He removed his hat and placed it on the arm of the sofa.

"I'm tired." She admitted.

"Not sleeping again?" He raised an eyebrow at her, and she knew a lecture was likely running through his mind.

"Not the way I need to. And before you sing the praises of pharmaceuticals, I've started taking my sleeping pills again. They just aren't doing me any good."

He frowned. "Maybe it's time to talk to Dr. Yates again."

She shrugged and sat next to him. "I don't know. Lately it feels like I've been talking in circles."

He patted her arm. "I'm sure it can feel that way, but you've been making progress. Anything I need to know about?"

Macy battled with the option of telling him the truth about her hallucinations, but in the end she couldn't bring herself to admit it. He thought she was improving, and she didn't want to bust that bubble of hope.

She shook her head. "Nope. All is good."

He nodded. "Good. Good. Glad to hear it." He stood. "Can I see the progress on the painting?"

"Yes, absolutely." She made her way down the hall as he followed her.

Macy reached in and flicked on the light. She entered and said, "I've not changed a lot since you last looked at it, but it's still what I was feeling at the time. I still have some minor details to add, but otherwise I'm done."

She looked at the painting and stopped in her tracks. Someone had altered it from the last time she remembered working on it. The dark figure that lurked in the doorway of a dingy room was still visible, but there was another figure added to the room.

A girl. Someone had shackled her to the bed.

It wasn't well done. The strokes were sloppy and almost childish in execution. When did she add this? The housekeeper was on vacation and there'd been no one else in the house since she last remembered working on it.

Uncle Robbie cleared his throat. "Well, that's definitely darker than your last one. And I'd say that's a bit of a change from the other day." He stepped forward and leaned in close to inspect it. "What inspired this?" His voice was calm, but she sensed it unnerved him. His stance was tense.

"I don't really know." She was thankful she didn't have to lie about that. Macy had no recollection of painting this addition, so she truly couldn't give him the muse behind it.

"Hmm. Well, it's interesting. Different." He gave her a sidelong glance. "Honestly, Ladybug, I'm not sure this will be to Mrs. Chase's liking."

Macy shrugged, too puzzled by the addition to care about Mrs. Chase's preferences. "If she doesn't mind waiting a little longer, I can try to start another. This is just what came out, same as usual… mostly."

"You're the artist." He continued to look it over.

It wouldn't be that hard to fix, but she couldn't allow her subconscious self to sabotage her work this way. She'd lose commissions if this continued.

"I can fix it. Don't worry. I'll do my best to put it back the way it was last time you saw it. Mrs. Chase will love it."

He smiled. "Wonderful."

Macy tucked her hair behind her ears as she continued to study the work before her. She knew she zoned out at times, but completely forgetting that she'd painted something was definitely out of the norm.

Her uncle patted her on the back. "It'll be amazing. Your work always is."

She nodded again, lost in thought.

His phone pinged, and he looked at the screen. "I need to call a client, mind if I use your office?"

She waved him away. "Sure, whatever you need."

He put the phone to his ear as he walked away.

Macy started mixing the colors she'd need to paint over the newest strokes. Once content with her plan, she picked up a brush and got to work.

She didn't know how long she'd been painting when her uncle interrupted.

"Looking much better." He smiled as he stood behind her.

"I think so too." She cleaned a brush. "I think another hour or two and I'll be done."

He nodded in appreciation. "Send me a photo when you're done. I'll send it to Mrs. Chase."

"Sure thing." She wiped her hands on a towel next to the canvas. "Are you leaving now?"

He looked at his watch. "I'm not in a hurry, if you want me to hang around."

"I'd love to get this painting in her hands as soon as possible. I don't have much left, then we need to let it dry. Want to watch a movie when I'm done?" She feared if she kept the painting, she'd end up vandalizing her work again. She felt sure they could transport it to her uncles to dry, if they were careful.

His brows drew together. "Doesn't it need to dry longer?"

"Yes," she replied. "But if we load and unload it carefully, it can dry at your place."

"Why?" His gaze was skeptical.

She sighed. "Because I've been feeling off lately. I just feel like it's safer with you."

"I don't understand. Why would the painting be in danger?"

Macy didn't want to tell him. She didn't want to explain what had been happening lately. "Just trust me on this. It's better off with you."

He nodded, but she knew he would push for answers later.

She finished the painting and brought it to the living room. It was comforting to see it finished, and she wanted it in her sight until her uncle took it with him.

She popped some corn and started a movie. Her uncle sat next to her on the sofa, laughing at the antics on screen. Macy couldn't tear her eyes from the painting. She couldn't get past an irrational fear that if she diverted her eyes for even a minute, it would change on her again.

13

ROBERT

Robert McCall sat at his desk and poured over some last-minute information that had come in for a client he was representing in the morning. It was late, and the day was catching up with him, but it wasn't uncommon for him to burn the midnight oil when a situation called for it. He'd been working from dusk til dawn the last few days. He'd had to cancel dinner with Macy two nights in a row, but he'd rather do that than not be available for her during the weekday.

A knock on his office door startled him. "Who's there?"

The door opened to reveal Macy standing on the other side.

He put a hand on his chest. "Mercy, girl. You about gave your old uncle a heart attack. What are you doing out at this hour?" He turned his gaze back to the paper he'd just written a note on.

She entered and shut the door behind her. "I needed to talk to you."

He looked up at her and nodded. "Okay." He organized the papers and tucked them into a manilla folder. "Now,

Ladybug, what was so important that you couldn't call? We could have talked after your appointment in the morning."

She sat in the chair in front of his desk and crossed her legs. "Did you look through all those photos you took home?"

He tried to stifle an automatic frown. "I did. Why?"

"I found them enlightening." She stated flatly.

He cleared his throat. "In what way?" He moved some folders around on his desk, working to hide the very photos she'd mentioned.

She leaned forward and placed her hands on the desk. Robert didn't like the look in her eyes. Something wasn't right. "Some of those photos were a little… different from the others, were they not?"

He leaned back, instinct telling him to put space between them. "I don't catch your meaning." He stuttered. "T-t-they are all from the old house. Your mom, dad, various people that worked for the family. You."

She stood and walked to a photo on the wall. It was a photo of Robert and her father. She pulled it off the nail and showed it to him. "Happier times." She ran a hand over the glass. "Do you miss him?"

"Do I miss your father? My only brother? Of course I do. What kind of question is that?" The insinuation insulted him.

"Oh, I don't doubt you miss him. But I'm sure there are people you don't miss. People you are glad to be rid of forever." She continued to study the photo.

Robert stood and rubbed the bridge of his nose. "Macy, I don't know what game you are playing here, but it's late and I'm tired."

She raised the frame above her head and smashed it on the corner of his desk, fragments of wood and glass sailed in different directions. "You are the one playing games, Robert!"

He stepped back, the horror of her outburst obvious on his face. He'd never seen her like this. When she was a teen, she'd had some anger issues, but nothing so volatile that she'd gotten physical. This wasn't like her at all. He wondered if her medications had somehow backfired. Or if she was having some kind of manic episode.

He held up his hands in front of him. "Macy, I promise you I'm not playing games. I honestly don't know what you are talking about."

She wiped the glass fragments from her hands, leaving small smears of blood behind as the smaller slivers cut into her skin. "You know my father wasn't the man he pretended to be. None of my family really was."

Robert cleared his throat. There's no way she could know about that. Was it genetic? She certainly behaved more like… No. He wouldn't entertain the thought.

Macy stepped closer. "He had a lot of secrets, didn't he Robert?"

She was oddly calm now, and that worried him almost as much as her earlier tantrum.

"Macy, we all have things in our past we'd like to forget. I'm sure your father was no different." He straightened his tie.

She laughed. "Is that we're calling it? Just something we'd like to forget?"

"Macy, I don't know what you think you know, but let me assure you that your father was a good man. Your mother was a remarkable woman. Don't dare sully their names." He used his court voice, hoping that'd put an end to this conversation.

She shook her head. "He had one specific dirty little secret, though. One you helped him cover up."

Robert felt the blood drain from his face. "No. That's incorrect."

"Liar!" She shouted.

"I…" he looked around, unsure what he needed to say or do.

"Did you ever tire of pretending?" She took a step toward him.

He stepped backward. "We'd both made mistakes in our lives. We had each other's backs. That's what brothers do."

"A mistake. Is that what he called it?" She glared at him.

Robert stared at Macy. There is no way she could know. There were only a handful of people that knew about that problem, and all but him had passed in the fire.

Macy sat back down in the chair she'd previously vacated with no regard for any frame debris that may have landed there. "You should really think of ways to make this right. If you were looking at this objectively, how would you demand recompense?"

He frowned. "Macy, there is no reason to atone for anything."

"So you keep saying." She picked up a large round shaped paperweight from his desk and tossed it around in her hands.

"Are you feeling okay? You don't seem quite yourself tonight?" He needed to understand this line of questioning.

"I'm just fucking peachy." She looked at her fingernails, boredom marring her expression.

"You're upset. You only curse like that when you're upset. Tell me what brought all this on."

She sighed and raised her eyes to his. "Maybe I'm tired of secrets and lies. I'm tired of having to fight to get to the truth every… damn… day."

"Honey, I don't know what's happening here. If you want

to talk about it tonight, we can. Otherwise, can we maybe discuss this tomorrow, when I've had some sleep and can think properly?"

She smiled at him and stood. "That'll be fine, Uncle Robbie. I'll let you rest. It looks like you need it."

He stepped over the mess on the floor and pulled her in for a hug. "Let's talk tomorrow after your appointment. I'll order us some lunch this time. Sound good?"

She smiled and nodded at him. "Of course."

He hoped he could explain away anything she thought she'd discovered. Maybe he could convince her that her paranoia was creating odd ideas in her head. It probably wasn't far from the truth. Either way, his brother had convinced him to help with a serious problem, and he'd done his best, right or wrong. That problem had been laid to rest a long time ago and needed to stay that way.

14

MACY

Macy knocked on her uncle's office door. He'd promised to pick her up after her session, but he wasn't waiting at the bus stop. He'd planned to take her home before his first case of the morning.

"Uncle Robbie? You in there?" She knocked again.

After a moment of silence, she tried the doorknob. It turned easily, and it surprised her he'd left it unlocked. He always locked his office when he was away.

Macy pulled out her cell phone and dialed his number. She heard his familiar ringtone come from inside the office.

She pushed open the door slowly until it was all the way open. Her screams echoed down the hall as she saw the bloody mess on the desk, floor, and walls.

Robbie's colleague Jared came running from a nearby office. "What's wrong, Macy?"

She stood there, unable to move. Her lip quivered as she stared at the dress shoes barely peeking out behind the desk on the floor.

Jared's eyes must have followed hers. "Oh, shit!"

She heard him move slightly, then say, "Yes, get an ambulance and the police here as soon as possible."

His words sounded as if they were coming from somewhere far away. Like yelling through a tunnel or underwater. Her vision blurred, and she leaned against the doorjamb for support.

"This can't be happening." She whispered to herself. "God, no. Please don't let this be real." She closed her eyes tight and took four deep breaths before opening them again.

It was all still there. The blood. Uncle Robbie's body. She wasn't dreaming, and it wasn't some kind of twisted hallucination.

Jared pushed past her and cautiously entered Robbie's office. As he rounded the desk, his eyes widened and his hand flew up to cover his mouth. He leaned down and Macy lost sight of him for a couple of minutes. When he stood back up, his hand was bloody and shaking.

Jared stepped back out of the office, using his handkerchief to clean his hand. He tugged her away from the door. "You don't need to see any more of that." He pulled her in for a hug. "The police are on their way."

"Is he...?" She couldn't bear to finish the question.

"Yes, he's gone." Jared replied softly. "I'm so sorry."

She buried her face in his shirt and openly sobbed. Robbie was the only family she'd had left. He'd been the person she'd relied on since she was a girl. Now she'd lost him too, and she was truly alone.

He took her to his office and sat her on a small leather sofa near the window. "Stay here. I'm sure the police will want to speak with you once they arrive, so I'll bring them to you."

She nodded.

He handed her a box of tissues. "I'll be back in a few minutes. Will you be okay?"

She nodded again and blew her nose.

He slipped out the door and Macy sobbed quietly, the loss something she felt in her soul. Her uncle had been nothing but kind to her. He'd raised her, protected her, and assured she'd want for nothing. Even as an adult, she needed him. How could she continue on alone?

She watched out the window for several minutes, her mind taking her to places she'd rather not remember. The funeral for her family was almost unbearable. Seeing her parents laid to rest on the same day would make any child depressed. But then there were the services for her nanny, the housekeeper and her daughter, and a couple of her dad's associates who'd been having a late-night meeting at the house when the fire broke out.

She snapped into focus on the present as she saw the police and what she assumed was the medical examiner pull up in front of the building.

Macy wiped her eyes and sat stoically as she waited for them to talk with her.

Moments later, Jared entered the room and a gray-haired man in a brown suit and tie followed him.

"Hi Macy, I'm Detective Asher. It's nice to meet you, although I'm sorry it's under these circumstances." He sat in a chair next to the sofa, giving her plenty of space.

"Yeah, me too." She sniffed and wiped her nose.

"Can you tell me everything that happened when you got here today?"

She shrugged. "Not much to tell. Uncle Robbie was supposed to take me home today after my doctor appointment. I called him, but he wasn't answering. So I took the bus here and figured I'd wait until he was done with whatever business was keeping him."

Detective Asher took notes as she spoke.

"I got off the elevator, knocked on his door, but there was no answer. So I called again, and that's when I heard his phone from inside the office." She looked him in the eye. "He never goes anywhere without his phone. I got worried and opened the door. That's when…" She took a deep breath. "That's when I saw him on the floor. And all the blood." Another stream of tears fell.

"So, the door was shut, but not locked?" He asked.

She nodded. "Correct."

An officer opened the door and approached the detective. He leaned into his ear and whispered something.

Detective Asher nodded. "Good, that'll help." He addressed Macy once again. "Do you know of anyone that would have wanted to hurt your uncle?"

She shook her head. "I'm sure he probably has an angry client or two. He is… was an attorney, after all. But personally, I can't think of a soul who'd do something like this."

He cleared his throat. "Were you aware that he'd had some death threats in recent months?"

Macy's eyes widened. "No. He never mentioned it."

"According to a receipt on his desk, he'd had a hidden camera installed in his office. Possibly as a precaution. It sounds like he was worried something would happen. He never hinted at possibly being in danger?"

This news floored Macy. She'd had no idea this was happening. Guilt flooded through her. He'd been so busy taking care of her, he neglected his own problems. Or at least he kept them away from her.

"No, he never said a word about it." She wiped away another tear.

"We'll look at the video and see if the camera caught anything important."

Jared sighed and interrupted. "I told him he needed to go to the police with the threats. He said they were harmless. Then he installed the camera, which I told him was a bad idea unless he planned on meeting clients elsewhere or disclosing that he was recording them."

Detective Asher moved his gaze from Macy to Jared. "Do you know where the camera is hidden?"

Jared nodded. "Yes, I can show you."

The detective stood. "Miss McCall, if you think of anything else that might be important, please don't hesitate to call me." He handed her a card.

She tucked the card into her purse. "I will. Thank you."

She went downstairs and Troy met her at the entrance door to her uncle's building, his face drawn and sad. "I'm so sorry, sweetheart. One of your uncle's friends called me to come get you. Jared, I think. I came as soon as I could."

She stood on the sidewalk and cried in his arms, giving no regard to those walking around them.

She was unsure how long they'd been standing there, but his comfort was short lived.

"Macy McCall. You're under arrest for the murder of Robert McCall." Detective Asher yanked her away from Troy and pulled her hands behind her back.

"What?" She asked through her tears.

Troy stepped forward. "Wait, you can't do that."

A uniformed officer stepped in front of him. "Stand back kid, or you'll go to jail too."

Troy shouted. "She didn't do anything wrong."

Macy was in a daze. So much had happened already, and now this.

An officer read her her rights, then he tucked her into the

back of a police car as dozens of onlookers watched with interest.

Troy raised his voice. "I'll get you a lawyer, Macy. Don't worry. We'll sort this out."

She could do nothing but nod. She'd gone from grieving to numb. And now she was soon to be confined to a cell she couldn't escape from. Her worst nightmares were coming true.

*M*acy sat in a gray room that was barely big enough for its table and three chairs. They had left her in there for what felt like hours. Her anxiety had increased so much that there were points where she thought she'd collapse or her heart would give out. The thumping in her ears was so loud that by the time the detective and her lawyer arrived, she could barely register what they were saying.

"Can I have a moment with my client?" Jared asked. He glanced at her clammy skin. "And a glass of water, please. She suffers from PTSD and anxiety. This room is making it worse."

The detective nodded and stepped outside.

Jared looked her in the face. "Macy, can you hear me?"

She shifted her eyes to his face, but struggled to concentrate on his words.

The detective knocked and came back in with a bottle of water.

"Thank you." Jared handed the water to her. "I don't know if this helps, but focus on taking small sips. Maybe try to ground yourself before we chat."

She registered the suggestion and forced herself to concentrate on the bottle. Water. She needed to sip the water.

Once she'd taken a couple of small drinks, she felt a little better. Jared's presence was also helping. Someone she knew had come to her rescue.

"Are you better?" He asked.

She nodded. "I think so." She whispered.

"Okay, good." He took a deep breath. "We are in a bit of a pickle here, Macy." He pulled a few photos from his briefcase. "They pulled these stills from the hidden camera in your uncle's office."

She looked at the photos he slid across the table for her inspection. The top photo made her gasp. It wasn't super clear, but it appeared to be her. She was standing over her uncle's dead body, a large object in her hand. Blood covered the object.

She shook her head. "No. No. No. No. Noooo." She pushed the photos away, her tears filling her eyes. "That's not me, Jared. Please, believe me."

He pressed his lips together. "It sure looks like you. The video shows you arguing with him, then bashing his head in with a large paperweight from his desk."

"But I didn't!" Panic filled her chest.

"That's going to be hard to sell. Our only saving grace here is that it's hard to see this person's face. Do you have an alibi for that evening?" He looked at her. He didn't hold an ounce of confidence in her story. She could see it.

"I… I do, actually. Troy and I were shopping. We'd made a last-minute plan to get my groceries for the week. By the time we'd gotten home, I was exhausted. We made some tea, then I napped on the sofa while we watched a movie. He was with me all night."

He studied her a moment. "So if that's true, who is this?" He jabbed his finger into the photo.

Macy swallowed hard. Would he believe her? "I don't know. I've been seeing someone that looks just like me lately."

He cocked his head to one side. "So your saying you have a twin?" Jared's head shook slowly.

"I don't know. I just know I didn't do that. Uncle Robbie meant the world to me. You know that. You wouldn't be here if you believed I was guilty." She prayed she was right.

Jared scooped up the photos and stuffed them back into his case. "I'll get your story verified. Hang tight and do your best to remain calm until I can get you out of here. I'll be back as soon as I can."

She nodded. "Thank you."

He left without another word. Macy spent the next hour or so in silence, her mind racing. She didn't know how it was possible. She felt sure she hadn't left last night. Troy could vouch for her, couldn't he? She prayed he could.

Jared and Detective Asher entered the room. Asher looked annoyed. "You're free to go, Miss McCall."

Jared smiled at her. "Your alibi checked out. We have multiple witnesses at the grocery store, plus Troy swears he was with you until this morning. He even remembers getting up to get some water around the time of your uncle's death. He swears you were fast asleep. Snoring away."

She cried with relief.

"Miss McCall." Detective Asher addressed her. "I don't know what's going on here, but something stinks and I intend to find out what it is."

"I hope you do." She breathed. "I'd like to know the answers myself."

The detective nodded. "Don't take any sudden vacations, in case we need to speak with you further."

"Not a problem. You know where to find me." She blew her nose as Jared led her from the room. When they exited the building, Troy was pacing outside the doors.

"Macy! Thank God!" He pulled her close and held her.

She pulled back and addressed both men. "Thank you. Both of you."

Jared nodded, but looked uncomfortable. "I will do my best to get to the truth Macy, whatever that may be."

"Good." She meant it, even if that truth was that she'd had actually killed her uncle. She felt deep down that she wasn't guilty, but it was hard to be one hundred percent confident when she was seeing things she shouldn't and losing time so often.

"You've got my number. Let me know if anything comes up. Meanwhile, I'll keep digging." Jared shook Troy's hand and walked away.

"He thinks I did it." Macy tried to hide the hurt in that revelation.

"Well, there is video." Troy stated.

"You think I killed my uncle?" The hurt turned to despair.

"No, I don't. I don't believe you're capable. But you have to admit it's damn weird."

She leaned into him, and he put his arm around her. "You saw me sleeping. All night?"

He nodded. "Most of it, anyway. I mean, I slept too so I can't say that you didn't get up to pee or something, but I'd have known if you'd left for more than a few minutes at a time."

She hugged him close. "I don't know how I'd get through my crazy life without you."

Troy kissed the top of her head. "Let's go home."

$\mathcal{M}$acy walked into the house in a daze. She'd spent the entire car ride home trying to process the events of the day. All she wanted was to disappear. Her body moved as if on autopilot, with no cognizant thinking on her part.

She shuffled up the stairs and into her bedroom. She dropped her purse and sweater on the floor as she made her way to the bed. It creaked under her weight as she flopped down on the mattress, her arms straight out to her side. Macy pulled her legs up to her chest and rolled to one side, pulling her arms in as well. She grabbed the blanket and balled it up, pressing it to her chest.

"Macy?" Troy stood in the doorway. "Are you going to be okay?"

Her eyes stung once more and tears filled her lashes before dropping to her cheeks. Her voice was soft as she tried to answer him. "I don't know if I'll ever be okay again."

He sat next to her on the bed and placed a hand on her back, stroking it. "What can I do?"

She sat up and turned to face him. "I don't know what's happening, Troy? I don't know who or what I am anymore?"

Tears continued to flow as she let her grief take over. "He's gone and I'm sure I didn't do it, but..." she gripped Troy's shirt in desperation. "How is it possible? How? That video was me, Troy. How can that be?"

He put his hands on either side of her face, forcing her to focus on him. "Macy, you were with me, right here. Unless you snuck out, got a cab to drive you miles into the city, did the deed, and then took another cab back, all while changing clothes and disposing of the bloody ones without a trace, it couldn't have been you. And I was awake most of the evening. You did not leave."

He pulled her to him, and she shifted, laying her head in his lap. He again lightly rubbed her arms and back.

She wanted to believe him. But he loved her. What if he was lying to protect her? What if she had left, and he didn't want to admit it? It's hard to see the worst in the people you love. For his own sake, he needed to get away from her. He needed to save himself. Being associated with a murder suspect would not be good for his career, and it couldn't be good for his mental health. The stress alone had to be hard on him.

If she loved him, and she believed she did, she needed to set him free. He deserved a life without the black cloud that plagued her's.

She couldn't do it today. She didn't have the energy, but she'd have to cut him loose. It would break her even further, but this wasn't about her needs anymore. She had to think of what was best for him.

"Tomorrow." She whispered, not realizing she'd said it out loud. She'd closed her eyes, enjoying the tender way he cared for her, knowing she wouldn't have many more opportunities to appreciate how amazing he was.

"What about tomorrow?" He asked, stroking her hair.

Macy didn't open her eyes. "I think we should talk about it tomorrow."

She felt the back of his fingers as they grazed her cheek. "That's a good idea. We'll figure out tomorrow. Tonight, you just need to rest."

She didn't care that they were talking about different solutions. Tonight she'd pretend they would be okay. She needed to believe it, if just for a little while longer.

15

DANIEL

aniel sat at his desk and waited for Macy to arrive. He had the general practitioner's notes in front of him and they had a lot to discuss.

A knock at the door signaled her arrival. "Come in, please."

Macy entered quietly, her expression drawn and subdued.

"How are you?" He took a seat across from where she normally sat.

She shrugged. "I don't know." She brushed something from her eye. He suspected it was tears.

He studied her a moment. She had the look of someone in shock. Numb. Numb was dangerous.

"Did Troy bring you today?" He hoped bringing up her boyfriend would bring her some joy. It failed.

She nodded, but said nothing more.

"We need to discuss your MRI results. Are you up for that?"

She looked at him then. "Yes."

He flipped through the paperwork he had in his hands. "So, as your doctor should have already explained, they found nothing abnormal in the scans. That's good news. No tumors or growths that could cause your blackouts."

She nodded. "Yeah, that's good."

He tried a different tactic. "How are you feeling, overall?"

She looked down at her hands, and he noticed a lack of her normal fidgeting. She was stone still.

"I guess I'm grieving." She replied. "And I don't know what's real anymore." She adjusted in her chair. "I don't have a physical reason for the blackouts. I'm seeing someone who isn't there. And I'm doing things, horrible things, that I can't remember, yet I'm also not doing them." Her volume rose a little as she vented her frustration. "What the fuck is wrong with me, Dr. Yates?"

He raised a hand. "Hold on. Let's address these one at a time."

She nodded. "Fine."

"There are no physical reasons for your blackouts… that we know of. So the next explanation is there is possibly something going on in your hippocampus." He pointed to the side of his head. "This is one of four major areas believed to control memory function. Somehow, you seem to experience these dissociative episodes. You aren't physically blacking out or collapsing, so something is causing you to act, then forget that action. More like a transient global amnesia."

He paused, and she appeared to process that information.

"We don't suspect epileptic seizures or even psychogenic seizures. So my next train of thought is that we discuss your dissociative behavior."

She adjusted in her seat. "Okay."

"It could be possible that you've developed another identity. One that's trying to protect you."

Macy pressed her lips into a thin line. "You mean dissociative identity disorder."

He nodded.

"If that's the case, it's going about it all wrong. It feels like it's trying to ruin my life, not make it better." She bit her lip and popped her head up to look him in the eyes. "How do I live with this?"

"There are plenty of people that live happy lives despite D.I.D." He wanted to assure her they could get her through this. He heard an uncomfortable amount of desperation in her voice.

She stood, agitation framed her every step. "Have any of those people had random sex, or told off a friend, or…" she stopped. With a shaky hand she rubbed her face. "Have any of them had an identity that killed someone?"

He expected this question, yet it was still hard to answer. "Some have done a lot of things and of course they aren't happy with their alters afterwards." He stood in front of her now. "Violence isn't something I've seen from an alter, that's true. And I'm frankly thankful for that. But you need to remember two points. One is that we don't know yet if you have an alter, it's just a theory. And two, there is proof you didn't kill your uncle."

She closed her eyes and shook her head. "There's also proof I did. Which do I believe?"

Daniel nodded. He knew this was difficult for her to reconcile. "The police had substantial enough evidence to let you go, despite the video. The face of the murderer wasn't visible enough for an identification. If they really believed you'd done it, I think you'd be behind bars right now."

She sat back down, weariness taking over her features. "I have an amazing lawyer."

"You do. One that knew how to prove you could not have been in two places at once." He hoped that satisfied her. "And your alter, if you have one, couldn't have separated from your body and set out on its own."

She shook her head and appeared as if she might get sick.

Macy jumped up. "I need to go."

He looked at his watch. "Your session isn't over."

"I know, but I'm not feeling well. Can we pick up where we left off next week?"

He admitted she looked like she could use some sleep. "Go get rest, Macy. Don't let this torture you. I will help you figure it out."

She nodded. "Thank you." And with that, she left his office.

He sat at his desk and made some notes about her visit, then put his head in his hands. He wasn't sure what to think about her situation. He couldn't wrap his mind around her hurting anyone.

His head hurt. *Damn, he needed a good night of rest.*

*D*aniel sat at dinner, picking at his plate. The mystery surrounding Macy had preoccupied his mind all day. There was an important piece missing, and he worried if he didn't figure it out soon, she'd snap.

He was seeing signs that alarmed him. She was more subdued than normal. Her primary source of support, besides Troy, was gone, possibly by her own hands. While they had temporarily cleared her on a technicality, he wasn't sure how long before something else happened. Macy felt lost and was drowning in a sea of self-doubt. The progress she'd made was quickly fading under the shadow of recent events.

If she remembered, or even slightly believed, that she'd killed Robert McCall, she'd never forgive herself. Her guilt was already at an all-time high. This could be what pushed her over the edge.

"Am I boring you?" Sarah asked. Her smile only partially genuine.

"No, not at all. So sorry. I'm just… preoccupied today." He took another bite of his food, thankful she'd agreed to a night in. They'd been seeing a lot of each other since that first date, and she was important to him.

"So, what's on your mind? I'm not a therapist, but I can listen as good as one." She winked at him.

He wiped his mouth. "It's not really something I can talk about."

She stood, picking up her plate and he did the same. "It's a patient matter."

"Ah, I see." She rinsed the dishes off and began loading his dishwasher. "Can you be super vague?"

He smiled. "Well, let's just say I'm concerned about a patient's well-being. This person has been through so much and you don't know how they'll handle major upsets in their lives. They've just suffered a personal loss."

"Oh." She frowned. "That's so sad."

He nodded. "Yeah."

Sarah finished loading the dishes and then took his hand and led him to the sofa. "Okay, so what can you do for this patient to help?" She placed a hand over his.

Daniel sighed. "The usual. Have loved ones check in on them. Make sure she knows I'm here and that she has the correct resources if there is an emergency."

"Her?" Sarah asked.

"Ah, sorry. I can't get more specific than that. I probably shouldn't have even said that much." He frowned.

"I understand." She paused and studied his face for a moment. "Can I ask you something?"

Daniel squeezed her hand. "Probably."

She smiled. "You tease."

"What do you want to ask?" He softly ran his thumb over the back of her hand.

"When I stayed over the other night, you had a nightmare. You brushed it off as nothing, but you mentioned Vanessa. Is there more to this story than you've told me?"

He noticed she seemed nervous asking such a personal question. It was hard to answer, but maybe it was time he told someone, and she was now among the small group of people he trusted.

"Vanessa is the reason I became a psychologist." He cleared his throat. "She struggled with depression all her life. I now suspect there may have been some other undiagnosed issues as well, but depression was her biggest symptom."

Sarah smiled at him. "That's very sweet of you. You wanted to help her?"

He nodded. "I did. I was working on my undergraduate degree when the accident happened. She'd been showing signs of getting worse. She'd started refusing medications and insisted she could handle it all on her own. We'd just come home from a movie and it was raining. She suddenly spilled all her emotions out to me. How inadequate she felt, how she knew she'd never live a normal life, and she was sure she'd always be miserable. I tried to talk to her, but she just shoved everything I said back in my face. She even accused me of seeing someone else." He shook his head. "I wasn't of course, but she'd started developing paranoia and that was one of the things it had her believing."

"So she wasn't paying attention when she had the accident?" Sympathy laced Sarah's question.

"No. She was. For a second it seemed she had a moment of clarity. Then she told me she was so very sorry for what she had to do. She increased her speed, and I tried to calm her down. Then she jerked the steering wheel, and we hit the tree on purpose. It was essentially a murder/suicide mission. Only she failed. She was the only one that died that night. I survived, although sometimes I feel like I died with her."

A look of horror crossed Sarah's face. "Oh God. She tried to kill you both?"

He nodded. "I didn't put that in the official report. I think part of me didn't want to believe it, even though I'd witnessed it myself. Another part of me didn't want to sully Vanessa's name in any way. So saying she lost control of the car was easy to sell, under the circumstances."

Sarah pulled him close, and he gladly snuggled up to her, accepting and appreciating the comfort she offered. "You poor man. All this time you've had to live with that."

He wrapped his arms around Sarah. "What about you? You live with the physical and emotional scars from your father." He shook his head. "That can't be easy… all the abuse you suffered through."

She shrugged. "I've decided my past would only mold me by making me stronger. No weakness. No more victimization." He noticed her jaw clench slightly and he wondered if that was anger or determination in her expression. "I hold the reins now. I'm controlling things. My scars are lines of motivation."

He smiled. "I wish I were as strong as you. I dream about it sometimes, like the other night. I dream I can change her mind. Make her stop. But in the end I wake up and she's still gone. I'm still crippled and alone."

Sarah tilted his face to hers and lightly kissed his lips. "Not alone, Daniel. Not anymore."

He deepened the kiss, more than ever thankful for Sarah.

16

MACY

*M*acy sat at her kitchen table and looked at a large envelope that had just arrived in the mail. The return address was hers, and she once again had no recollection of sending anything.

She opened the envelope and dumped the contents on her table. Photos slid from the package and on to the wooden surface.

She spread them out, realizing these were the photos Uncle Robbie had taken with him the night she saw her doppelgänger in the upstairs bedroom. How she once again ended up with them was a mystery.

Most of them were run-of-the-mill pictures that any family would have. Holidays, parties, family gatherings or special moments of one sort or another. But there were a few that she didn't recognize.

A couple were of rooms she'd never seen before. While their house was large, some would even categorize it as a mansion, she'd explored every inch of her home in her free time. And she'd had a lot of free time.

The only area prohibited to her was the basement. She

vaguely remembered wandering down there once. Her father had caught her and her mother gave her a scolding, telling her that the basement was dangerous and they forbid her for her own safety.

As a child, Macy didn't really understand how it could be dangerous, but her father put the fear of God in her before it was all said and done. And her uncle sealed her curiosity off with a stern lecture as well. It would have taken a significant act of courage to attempt that adventure again.

She couldn't remember what she'd seen while she was down there. She remembered it being poorly lit, and she was fairly sure she'd tripped over something. Outside of that, it was a blur.

Macy studied the odd photos, then turned them over. One photo had a small bed, a chair, and what looked like the edge of a TV was barely in frame. Someone had scribbled TREAT-MENT ROOM on the back.

She certainly didn't remember a treatment room. Who was so sick they required their own room?

She turned the photo back over in her hands, and a memory flashed in her mind.

A large metal door with a small window. She had tried to push a chair up against it so she could look through it, but before she could get up on the chair, she heard someone coming and then... blank. She was unsure what had happened next.

It didn't feel like a pleasant memory. Fear floated to the surface when she thought of the big, scary door. Maybe it represented something? She didn't know. But what she did remember was that because of the way they built the house, parts of it still stood… like the basement.

After all that had happened in the last few weeks, she needed answers. Now, with her uncle gone, she had no one to ask questions to. The house was the only connection left to her past.

Macy changed into jeans, a long-sleeve shirt, and a pair of boots. With the unusual photos, a bottle of water, her keys, and a flashlight stuffed into a small sling bag, she headed outside.

She exited the back door, checking she'd locked it behind her, then she took a few minutes to survey her back yard. This was going to be hard. She hadn't been back to the house since the fire. Uncle Robbie wouldn't allow it. And to be honest, she wasn't sure she'd ever wanted to revisit it, until now.

Macy took some deep cleansing breaths and repeated her affirmations in her head. She knew seeing the remains of her life before trauma would be hard, but she had to try.

She began walking into the trees, working to ignore the surrounding sounds. "It's only nature" she reminded herself as she stepped over branches and rocks. She was momentarily distracted by the fact that normal people enjoyed walks like this, especially on such a gorgeous day. She should smile at the wildlife, photograph the flowers, and enjoy the cool breezes. Instead, she mostly worried about something getting to her, although what she had no idea. It wasn't like she was hiking in bear country or would have to watch out for lions. She was walking the few acres of woods that stood between her new house and her old house. The worst thing she might see was a snake, and she was doing her best to be very careful where she stepped. Staying on the least cluttered paths she could find.

After some time Macy slowed in her tracks as she came upon the clearing where her old house stood. It was foreboding and ominous.

The sun shone brightly on its carcass, allowing beams of

light to break through the bones that once had contained complete walls, ceilings, and floors.

She stepped into the light, trying to enjoy the warming sensation on her skin. Instead, a shiver ran down her spine and nausea threatened to bring her to her knees. She closed her eyes and focused on pushing down the memories that attempted to overwhelm her.

She opened her eyes and forced herself forward. Each step felt like torture and tears pricked at the corners of her eyes. She had to confront this. Somehow, she knew her answers were here.

She'd made it as far as the garden in front of the house when it all hit her in a flash. Wave after wave of terrifying memories assaulted her.

She stumbled and had to stop, seating herself on the ground in front of the steps of the stately old home.

She could smell smoke. That's how it all started. Smoke and shouts from distant voices.

Her mother came running into her room. "Get up baby, we have to get out of here."

Macy sat up in bed, rubbing her eyes. "What's going on?"

Shouting filled the hallway, and then her room got hazy with smoke.

Her mother handed her a pair of slippers and a robe. "Here, put these on. Quickly. We have to get out of here."

Macy began to truly wake up then. Something terrible was happening.

A scream pierced the air, and her mother started crying. She pulled Macy close and through her tears said, "It's gonna be alright, baby. I promise."

"Mama, is it a fire?"

Her mother nodded.

"How do we get out?" Macy tried to sound brave and be strong for her mother, but this terrified her.

"We'll see if we can get out the window." Her mother shoved aside the curtains and pushed up the sash. It opened easily enough, but when she leaned out, she heard her mother curse. Her mother never cursed.

The smoke was getting thick now and she could feel heat that hadn't been there moments earlier. Macy remembered some things she'd learned about fires, so she ran to her bedroom door and shut it, then grabbed a blanked from a nearby chair and rolled it up, stuffing it under the door to block any further smoke.

"Good thinking," her mother said, a bit of pride in her voice. "My smart, beautiful girl."

Macy ran to where her mother still stood at the window. "How do we get down?"

Her mother shook her head. "I'm not sure yet. If we had to, we could jump, but there's not much to catch us below. We don't want to land on the bricks if we can help it."

Macy heard another shout, this time closer to their door.

"Macy! Are you in there?" It was her father.

"Yes, Daddy! We're here!" She screamed at the top of her lungs.

Her mother ran to the door. "Brian! We have no way down!"

He kicked open the door and rushed inside. "We'll get out of here." He gathered his family in his arms as he looked around the room. "We have to find a softer place to jump from. I think if we land in the hedges it won't be so bad." He grabbed the blanket Macy had put under the door and ran to her bathroom. Once he'd soaked it in water and wrapped his wife and daughter up in it, he ushered them into the hall.

"Susan, if we can get to our room, I think we can safely

land somewhere on the east side of the house where all the bushes are."

Macy froze. In front of them, almost unbearable heat assaulted her skin. Flames had climbed the walls and were snaking across the ceiling at alarming speeds.

"We have to go." Brian shouted. He ushered his family in the opposite direction, the flames closing in from that side too. They reached her parents' bedroom, and he pushed open the door. The blanket that surrounded them was drying in places, as if the heat was already evaporating all the moisture from the fabric.

"Mommy?" Macy's terrified voice reached her parents. She watched in horror as the scene behind them unfolded. Something from the ceiling fell and landed on her father. He screamed in agony as the burning debris pinned him to the floor.

"Daddy!" Macy screamed and lunged to help her father. Susan grabbed Macy and shoved her into their bedroom with the orders "Get out any way you can. Even if you have to jump." She slammed the door in Macy's face.

Terror kept her from moving. Was her father okay? What was going to happen to her mother? Would they all die?

She turned in the room and remembered what her father said about the bushes. She ran to the window and checked that it was unlocked, then gave it a shove upwards. It wouldn't budge. She tried again. Nothing.

Macy ran to the door and shouted. "Mommy, the window won't open."

All Macy could hear was the roar of the flames. Smoke billowed under the door, filling the room. She coughed and fell to her hands and knees, crawling back to the windows. Despite her best effort, none of them would open.

The flames were licking the underside of the door now.

She knew if she didn't do something soon, it would be too late. Macy found a small statue of some man she knew nothing about. It took both hands to pick it up, but she carried it to the window and began smashing out the glass. By the time she'd made a hole big enough to escape through, the glass had sliced her hands in several places.

Heat crawled up her back, and she knew her time was up. Jumping still scared her, so she grabbed a bed sheet and tied it to a dresser near the window. She didn't think it'd hold, but maybe it'd last just long enough to make the fall less painful. Macy pushed the sheet out of the window, then carefully slipped through as well, only getting cut a few times on the way out. She used the sheet to lower herself down, but it slipped and she fell a couple of feet before slamming up against the outside of the house.

Flames from the window directly below her seared her stomach and she screamed, instinct making her let go of the sheet. She fell. And while it was only seconds before she hit the bushes below, in her mind it seemed like she'd fall forever.

The impact knocked the wind out of her and she doubled over as she rolled through the prickly branches and onto the grass. Her leg hurt badly, and she feared she'd broken it. She screamed in pain as she scooted backwards away from the house, dragging the injured leg.

In horror, she watched as every room on the upper level became an inferno. In the room next to her parents, she saw movement in the window and for a flash she'd hoped her parents had made it out of the hallway.

Then she saw the terrified faces of their housekeeper, Miss Christy. Her daughter Brandy, only a year younger than Macy, clung to her mother's side. Christy banged on the window and screamed. She pushed and pulled and hammered against the glass, but it wouldn't budge.

Macy tried to stand. She had to find some way she could help, but her leg hurt so badly that she struggled to move. Standing was impossible on her own.

Christy finally found something to break the window, and she screamed for help.

Macy cried as she again tried to get up and collapsed to the grass beneath her.

Christy had now put Brandy in front of her and was breaking out more glass. Macy hoped they were going to jump, as she had. But the room behind them continued to increase in brightness, and in a flash they'd disappeared into the flames.

Everything was quiet now. The screams had ceased. All she heard was the roar of the flames and the cracking of timber as various parts of the house collapsed.

Macy watched her house burn as shock set in. She heard sirens in the distance. Voices and faces eventually surrounded her, asking her questions and giving her medical attention. But from that point on, her life felt like she'd walked around in a fog. A fog that contained the most horrifying realities she'd ever faced.

Macy raised her head, tears creating trails down her face. She didn't know if she could do it. *Could she find the courage to walk back inside that house?* She gave herself some time to calm, as always using breathing techniques to get her past the panic.

When the panic had passed, she stood and wiped her face, then pulled the photos and the flashlight from her bag. "Suck it up, Macy." She said to herself. "You need to figure this out."

She walked up the steps to the double front doors. One

hung from its hinges, the other stood open as if inviting her to enter. She knew this was dangerous. This structure wasn't likely solid in most places, if at all. But the stone parts of the house seemed to still be intact. Maybe that was all she needed to safely look around. She promised herself she wouldn't stay long and would only go to areas that felt sturdy.

With tentative steps, she entered the doors and looked around. The foyer, charred and dim, only received light from where windows once stood. A huge stairway stood in the middle, the steps damaged or missing. The handrails on both sides had burnt black and sunlight formed dotted spotlights on the landing above the first floor. Macy peered upstairs, but knew going up there safely was out of the question.

The basement. She felt sure she needed to go there. If she could get to the basement, maybe some of these odd memories would come back to her. Recalling some things randomly, with no context, was unnerving.

She made her way behind the staircase, carefully stepping over debris in her way. It was darker back there. The sun couldn't penetrate the interior walls as easily here, so she switched on her flashlight to aid in her exploration.

As she entered another small hallway, she heard a noise off to her right. She stopped and flashed the light to either side, praying she saw nothing, yet wanting to know what she'd heard. All was still a moment longer, then a rat scurried across the floor and she jumped back, hitting the wall behind her.

Dust and soot fell around her head, creating a filthy cloud that choked her. Macy stepped away from the wall and coughed, digging for her bottle of water in the bag. Once she'd downed a few gulps, she gave herself a moment to recover and look around.

"Damn rat." She muttered.

Her eyes fell on the door near the kitchen. That was the door that led downstairs. The door she was told never to open.

She tiptoed across the room until she got to an area where she had to step over some boards and remnants of dishes. Her balance was a little off, and she'd almost fallen once after tackling the small hill of debris.

On the other side, it was a clear path to the basement. She shined the flashlight around the kitchen and area she'd just left, assuring she was alone.

With trembling hands, she turned the latch. The big metal door swung open easily, revealing concrete stairs that descended into total darkness.

"Oh, God." She muttered.

Her heart sped up its beating, and she had to steady herself as a wave of dizziness threatened to engulf her. Macy shook her head. "I've come too far to go back."

She gripped the railing with her right hand, giving it a good shake to assure its sturdiness, then pointed the flashlight down the steps. With each step, she gripped the railing and flashlight like a vice. The beam of light stretched out before her, revealing only more steps, until finally she saw tile flooring.

It was yellow, old, and broken in places, revealing the concrete beneath. As her feet touched the last step, she moved the light to the surrounding room. It was huge. Almost as big as the entire lower levels. There were a few smaller rooms off to one side. She could see canned goods and common house-hold staples on shelves as she peeked through the doors. Other rooms were empty or stored furniture and trunks in them.

She approached one trunk and pushed open the lid. Inside, she found nothing but clothes and books. Another trunk had dishes and some random items that looked to be from someone's childhood.

The last trunk's lock had been busted, the padlock now hung from it loosely. On further inspection, she realized someone had cut it.

She lifted the lid and was shocked to find it full of her father's belongings. There were paper's he'd worked on for various research projects, most of the titles and information blacked out. She found a couple of old journals with his handwriting inside. And last, a metal box with the word PHOTOS written in black permanent marker on the top.

She tucked the journals in her bag and walked out of the room with the metal box in her hands. Curiosity got the better of her and instead of waiting to look through the pictures at home, she sat on the steps and quickly rifled through a few.

One photo caught her attention. It was the same room as in the other photo she had, but this time a young girl sat on the bed. Her dark hair covered her face and she wore a light pink dress. They'd shackled her arms and legs to the bedpost.

Macy covered her mouth. "What in the hell?" She whispered. "Just like my painting."

Another photo of the room showed her sitting at a small table, eating something from a bowl, her face sad and drawn. Her face. It was Macy's face as a child.

She stood and closed the lid on the box. She moved the beam of light around the room, searching for the door she knew existed in her memories. After a bit of searching, she found it. The door was wide open and inside Macy found the table, chair, and bed she'd seen in the photos. She also found the shackles still attached to the bed.

She reached out to touch them but thought better of it and drew her hand back as if it'd bite her. To her left was a large wardrobe, and she inspected what few contents remained.

Behind the two ragged shirts that still hung haphazardly on hangers, she saw light peek through a crack. There was also an odd smell surrounding her.

On closer inspection she learned the crack was a door, the latch inlaid in the wood making it hard to find.

Macy stuffed the box into her bag, the end of it sticking out, then she shined the light on the indention, apprehension filling her veins as she worked up the courage to open it.

With trepidation, she pushed the door open and stifled a scream.

MACY

The smell of must and something she couldn't pinpoint hit her first, and it was all she could do not cough and gag. But the sight that greeted her was something out of a nightmare. There was a small window at the top of the room that had once been blacked out, but the fabric had decayed and fallen away, allowing enough sunlight to keep the room illuminated. Dark splotches covered various surfaces; the walls, floor, tables and equipment. A table against one wall had an assortment of terrifying looking instruments of torture, most of them covered in what she was sure was blood.

A chair sat in the middle of the floor, wires coming from it at various angles, all connected to a box on the wall. Dust coated every surface. Someone had covered the chair with a white, dingy sheet. Large pools of blood formed black and rust colored stains in various spots on the fabric. Under the sheet… that's what made her scream. It appeared to be a body. The tips of male dress shoes poked out from under the hem of the material. A skeletal hand hung loosely from one side. A rat scurred by and Macy felt a shiver go up her spine. She was certain pests had fed on him for years.

"He was a bastard. I promise, no one missed him." The voice echoed behind her. She turned to see her double leaning against the wall near the dusty television in the prison-like bedroom.

It took Macy a moment to find her voice. Without looking behind her, she pulled the door shut and stepped out of the wardrobe.

"What do you mean?" She moved closer to the bed.

Her double smirked. "That's Dr. Britton. He was a sadistic asshole. He enjoyed torturing and beating the girl they kept down here."

"I saw the photos…" Macy's voice trailed off.

"Yes, those wonderful photos. I wondered how long it would take you to add two and two."

Macy looked around the room. "Why don't I remember this room?"

The double shrugged. "Who knows? Maybe you've blocked it out of your memories."

"I… was I locked up in here?" She knew the photos showed her in there, but her memories of the basement were so few. "I mean, if I'd been locked up here for any period of time, wouldn't I remember that?"

The double stood upright and stepped toward Macy, causing her to shrink back. "Funny how memories are so selective sometimes." She looked at the box Macy had sticking out of her bag. "Reminders, like photos and journals, help bring the truth to light, don't you think?"

Macy placed her hand on the bag. "I guess."

The double looked at her and frowned. "Take those home and look through them. Study them. Learn something."

Macy stood in place, unsure what to say next.

"Go!" Shouted the double and Macy ran for the door. She stumbled her way to the stairs, not caring that she could barely see them. She felt her way up the steps, missing one or two in her scramble to escape the basement and her hallucination. When she reached the top, she slammed the door behind her. Feeling less threatened, she then fumbled for the flashlight to assure she didn't hurt herself on the way out.

Her double's voice seemed to echo around her. "Learn something. Open your eyes!"

Macy shoved her way out of the double doors and behind her she heard a crash as the door that had barely been hanging on, fell from the frame.

She ran into the woods, not caring that there might be snakes or beasts, or hell, even ghosts. She'd take any of that over what she'd just seen.

She ran until she reached the clearing where her own home now stood. As she stepped on to the freshly mowed grass, she placed a hand on her stomach and inhaled fresh gulps of air. Then she thew up all over the lawn.

It took her a few minutes to get her bearings as she let the emotions of the last hour rush through her. She placed a hand to her side and felt the box.

With careful steps, she made it to her back door and unlocked it. Once locked behind her again, she went upstairs and headed straight for the bathroom.

She looked at her reflection in the mirror and released a humorless laugh. She had soot and dirt streaked on her face, arms, and in her hair. It covered her clothes, the dusty remnants of the house. She'd have to shower and burn the clothes. Somehow it felt like any part of that house being there, even ashes, would only invite more evil into hers.

She called Troy, her voice surprisingly calm.

"Hey, do you have time to come over this evening?" She slid open the glass door, leaned in, and turned on the shower.

"I can." He replied.

"Great. I'll make dinner. I need your help to figure something out."

"Sounds good. See you in a couple of hours then?" He asked.

"Perfect. See you then."

She pushed end, then stripped down to her underwear, putting her jeans, boots, and t-shirt in a trash bag. Then she removed her underclothes and stepped under the hot stream of water, letting the flow wash away as much of her stress as she could.

Her eyes moved to the bag sitting on the floor. She'd figure this out. As sick as it made her feel, she had to know the truth.

*M*acy and Troy sat at the kitchen table, her with a hot cup of tea and him with a soda, both looking through the photos.

"I can't believe what I'm seeing." He remarked. "I mean. It looks like they held you hostage down there at some point." He frowned. "You don't remember any of it?"

She shook her head. "Not much. I remember the door to the room and trying to look out the window. I remember seeing the bed and the television on. Everything else is blank."

He whistled as he flipped through one journal. "I don't even know where to begin with this. This is has to be at the very top of the fucked-up scale."

Despite being alarmed, she liked that he'd cursed again. Maybe he was becoming more comfortable around her, despite all that had happened.

"What do you mean?" She picked up another photo.

"Well…" He took a deep breath and read.

"My dearest daughter. I'm so sorry I had to put you through all this. I hope that one day you'll read these journals and understand why we did the things we did. It was for your own good, always. Not every method for healing you was fruitful, or maybe even advised, in retrospect, but we only wanted to help you get better. At this point it appears there is no 'better' for you. You continue to worry us. Your violent tendencies and lack of understanding may always be your downfall. I pray I'm wrong."

Troy flipped another page. "Did you know he mentions demonic possession in here?"

Macy frowned. "I don't get this. I do not remember this." She picked up another of his journals, shaking it in frustration. "I don't know who this man is! That's not the father I remember." She tossed it across the room.

Troy ran his hands through his hair. "This is all so bizarre. And you saw the room yourself?"

Bile rose to her throat as she remembered the secret room with the body in it. "Yeah, I saw a lot."

Did she tell Troy? They already suspected her of killing her uncle. What would people think if they knew of a rotting corpse in the basement? And did she kill that man years ago? Was that part even real?

She groaned and laid her head on the table.

Troy touched her shoulder. "Hang in there. There has to be something we are missing. Something that will make all this make sense."

She thought so too, but the more she concentrated on

finding it, the more she wondered if whatever happened to her in that basement created the messed-up person she is today.

"Troy…" she said tentatively. "What if… what if they tortured me in that basement? What if those memories are so completely horrible that I've repressed them, and this double I'm seeing is an alter ego of mine? Maybe she's someone I've made up to protect myself from the truth."

He looked at her. "You think that's what's going on?"

"I don't know. Dr. Yates mentioned it could be possible."

Troy frowned. "Are you… are you thinking of, ending things?"

She frowned. "I'm not sure being with me is the best thing for you, Troy. But I can't say I've decided on that."

"What? You're thinking of breaking up with me?" He stood quickly.

"Isn't that what you just asked me?" She didn't understand his defensiveness.

"No. I wanted to know if you were planning to kill yourself." He paced the floor.

"Troy, why would you think that?" She stood and tried to face him.

He turned his back to her. "I don't know. It's just that with everything happening, it might be overwhelming. I just want to make sure you're handling all this okay."

She looked at him for a long moment before responding. "I guess I'd be lying if I said it hadn't crossed my mind. But I'm telling you right now that I'm more angry than suicidal. I'm tired of no one believing me. I'm tired of not believing myself!"

"Macy…" Troy began, and she assumed he was about to issue an apology. She didn't want one. Not right now.

"I think you should leave." She said coldly.

"Macy, please. I didn't mean to overstep. I'm just worried about you."

She nodded. "I know. But right now I have a lot to process, and I think it's better if I do it on my own. I'll call you later."

His expression was a mixture of defeat and frustration. It was the same look he'd had when they'd fought at the party a few weeks back. How long ago that felt now. Like a lifetime. So much had changed since then.

"I'll call you. I promise." She added.

"Fine. I'll talk to you later." He skipped the usual kiss goodbye, and she didn't blame him. She was mad at him and herself. She needed to think, and he needed to give her space.

He left, and she locked up behind him.

In the kitchen, she picked up the journal she'd tossed on the floor and gathered up the other two that sat on the table. Her appetite gone, she grabbed her tea, warmed it up, and settled in on the sofa, prepared to read for the rest of the night.

She'd only made it halfway through the first journal when she felt her eyelids getting heavy. She leaned back and tried not to think of the disturbing things she'd read.

The next thing she knew, she was in the prison room, her leg shackled to the bed.

"Daddy! Daddy help me!" Her small voice didn't sound right. It was her twelve-year-old voice in her twenty-four-year-old body. She yanked at the chains and her ankle chaffed. She bent down to rub it and the door opened. Her uncle and father entered, with her doppelganger directly behind them.

"I'm so sorry, Macy. I hate that we have to do this again." Her father put on a pair of rubber gloves.

She jerked against the restraints once more.

Uncle Robbie drew closer and grabbed her wrists, securing them to the other restraints on the bed.

"No, daddy!" She cried.

Her doppelgänger laughed. "Better you than me."

She started at her twin. "I am you." She shouted.

The twin walked over and patted her father on the back. He looked at the twin and smiled. "Not this time, Macy." She taunted her.

Macy screamed as loud as she could. "We've sound-proofed this room. No one can hear you."

Macy shook her head. "No. No, this isn't right." She looked around the room. "This isn't real. I read this in the journals or… or… I saw something in the photos."

Her father frowned. "Macy, you were told never to come down here!" He shouted.

Her uncle hurried out of the room and slammed the door behind him.

"I'm sorry Daddy, please don't do this. Please. I promise I'll never come down here again."

Her twin laughed. "I'm sorry daddy, I'm sorry. Blah, blah, blah. You're such a baby."

"Shut up!" Macy hated her double. She'd done nothing but ruin her life. "You are the reason, I'm here!"

The double nodded. "Indeed, I am. And I'm not leaving until you've suffered and lost everything."

"Why?" Macy moaned.

Macy's father looked at her with a puzzled expression. "Because there's something wrong with you. We need to fix it." He stated flatly.

Her double perched on the side of a table now and elbowed Macy's father. "Maybe we should finally try that lobotomy, huh?"

He chuckled but shook his head. "No, there has to be a better cure than that." He walked over to the wardrobe and pushed the clothes aside. When he opened the door, Macy screamed.

She woke herself up screaming. It was dark out, but thankfully all her lights were still on. She sat upright and looked at her phone. "Oh shit. It's almost 2:00 a.m."

She had promised to call Troy before bed. She'd have to do it in the morning.

She gathered up the journals and sat them on the coffee table, then double checked the locks and went upstairs. She took her sleeping meds, praying they'd knock her out without nightmares, and went to bed.

The next morning she awoke to knocking. Persistent, annoying, knocking. She put on her robe and slippers and went downstairs. The knocking continued, followed by the occasional doorbell ring.

"Hold your damn horses." She shouted.

She cautiously opened the door to see a disheveled and angry Troy on the other side. She stepped aside and yawned.

"Sorry, I know I said I'd call you last night-."

He cut her off as he barged in. "But you figured filming a video was better?" He shook his head. "I'm sorry, Macy, but this was downright cowardly."

She ran her fingers through her messy hair. "What the fuck are you talking about?" She was tired, it'd been a hellish few days, and she wasn't in the mood for any of it anymore.

He held up his phone. "Don't pretend like you didn't do this. Or did your evil side do it?" He was sarcastic, and it instantly set her on edge.

"What did you just say to me?" Anger bubbled to the surface.

"Listen, I have stood by your side through this entire mess. There is absolutely no reason to attack me like this." He sounded hurt, but she didn't yet know what brought all this on. No matter, she was dangerously close to kicking him out on his ass.

"Here." He shoved the phone at her, a video on the screen.

She took the phone and pressed play. It was her, sitting in her kitchen, wearing the same thing she wore the evening before.

"Listen, Troy," the video said. "This isn't working. You aren't the support system I need. You can't be patient with me, you run off to God knows where for your job, and it's usually when I need you most. You can't be bothered to believe me when I tell you things I'm going through. And if I'm being completely honest, I think you're just after my inheritance." She leaned forward and frowned. "It's over. Thanks for nothing. Don't bother me again."

The video stopped.

She didn't know what to say. Again, she had no recollection of filming that. "Troy, I don't know what to say."

He nodded. "That's what I figured." He turned to leave. "You know, I really do love you. I was going to propose at Christmas. I had this whole grand gesture planned out. I'd even involved your uncle in the planning. But I'm glad I found out what kind of person you are before I jumped in that deep." Tears formed on his lashes.

"Take care of yourself, Macy. I hope you find the help you need." He stormed out, slamming the door behind him.

She stood in the foyer, stunned. When had she filmed that? Before or after her nightmare? She worried she might not be healthy for him. She'd even seriously considered breaking up with him a few times, but now that they were over, she felt empty. Broken. Hopeless.

She didn't want him to leave, but how could she argue with the proof they both saw?

She crumbled to the floor in a heap, tears flowing hard. Now she was truly and totally alone.

18

MACY

*L*ightning flashed outside, momentarily followed by the deep rumble of thunder. Macy flinched with each flash. It frayed her nerves to the point of snapping. This was not how she'd envisioned spending her Saturday night. Not that she'd had any plans at all since her breakup with Troy.

She pushed damp hair out of her eyes as she shuffled along the sidewalk, hoping she reached Dr. Yates' office before the sky opened up completely. She was already cold and soaked to the bone, but she'd never dry out if it continued to dump rain on her intermittently. It was moments like this that she really wished she'd learned to drive. The cab ride was miserable, and she'd finally snapped, making the poor guy drop her off before getting to her destination. The walk to Dr. Yates' office from three blocks away felt like an eternity.

She reached the building and blew out a sigh of relief. When she stepped inside, the thunder cracked once more, causing her to yelp.

"You okay, miss?" A young building security guard stopped in front of her and stared for a moment.

"Yes, thank you." She pointed up. "The thunder startled me."

He cleared his throat and nodded. "I understand. It's rather loud tonight."

Macy glanced outside. "It is."

"Can I help you? It's not usual business hours." He smiled.

"Oh, no thank you. I'm meeting Dr. Yates at his office." She adjusted her jacket.

He looked her over. "I see. Well, you have a good night then."

"You too." She replied as she walked to the elevators. The door slid open, and she slipped inside, pushing the button for the third floor.

As the doors closed, she saw an older security guard try to catch her attention. She pushed the door button but was too late to stop the movement. She ascended and figured if it were important, he'd come up to find her or call Dr. Yates' office.

The melodic tone of the elevator showed she'd reached her floor, and she hastily exited the confines of the elevator. Dr. Yates' office was at the end of the hall, which had always seemed inviting during the daytime. Tonight, she felt a sense of foreboding as she passed office after office. She wasn't sure why Dr. Yates needed to see her so urgently, but it couldn't be good. They hadn't had an appointment since her breakup with Troy, so she assumed he might be worried about her since she sent him a message about it. Maybe that would be their topic of conversation.

As she approached his office, she noticed his door open just a crack. With her hand on the knob, she knocked. No sound came from within, so she pushed the door open and entered.

"Dr. Yates? I'm here. Sorry it took me so long to get here." She looked around the room, noting that nothing there seemed out of the ordinary.

"Dr. Yates?" She called again.

The door shut behind her, and she spun to face it.

Sarah stood behind her. Macy instantly remembered the gorgeous blonde Dr. Yates had with him at the Brazilian steakhouse that night. She was one of those beautiful people that were hard to forget.

"Sarah, what are you doing here?" Macy tried to hide the discomfort seeing Sarah instigated. Macy knew nothing about her.

Sarah looked her over. "My, my. Aren't you a mess, Macy McCall?" She stepped around her and walked to stand behind Dr. Yates' desk.

Macy's hand flew to her hair. "Yeah, I forgot to grab an umbrella." Her cheeks heated at being so disheveled in front of someone that seemed so put together.

"Oh, I'm not talking about your appearance." She clicked the mouse on the desk and the computer hummed to life.

"You aren't?" This confused Macy. "Where is Dr. Yates? He said to meet him here."

"Did he?" Sarah sat in his chair.

Macy dug out her phone. "I have a text." She held the phone up as a confirmation of her statement.

"From Daniel? Are you sure?" Sarah retorted.

Macy looked at her phone, then back at Sarah. She repeated her original question. "Why are you here?"

Sarah smiled. "I thought it was time we had a chat."

Macy's discomfort increased. Something felt off.

"I know you hold affection for Daniel. I'm sure that's only increased since losing your boyfriend." Sarah pasted a mock frown on her face. "It must be hard to lose so many important people in such a short time."

Macy stepped back, trying to put some distance between her and Sarah.

Sarah pulled a bag from behind the desk. In moments, she'd unpacked several items. "You have lost a lot, haven't you?"

Macy nodded, her hand squeezing the back of a chair that she gripped for balance.

"I have too, you know. I've lost everything." She sighed as she used a wipe to clean makeup from her face. "Not that everything I had was worth much. I liked my mother, at first. My father was a tyrant who beat me mercilessly. I didn't measure up." She gave Macy a pointed look. "Do you ever feel you don't measure up?"

Macy couldn't speak as she watched Sarah's bizarre ritual of removing makeup. Mascara streaked both sides of her eyes now, and tilted downward like some kind of deranged clown.

"I think you do. More than you are willing to admit." Sarah stopped working on her makeup and worked on something around her nose.

With horror, Macy watched Sarah peel the skin from her nose until she revealed the latex fraud that covered her real nose.

A gasp escaped Macy's mouth as she saw the real woman beneath.

"Oh, it gets better." Sarah smirked at Macy, then leaned her head over and removed something from her eye. A bright blue contact sat on the tip of Sarah's finger. She held it out for Macy's inspection. "These things are amazing." She removed the second one and tossed them in the bag. "I don't think I'll need those anymore."

Macy struggled to find her voice. "You."

Sarah laughed as she put her hands in her hair and tugged, the blond wig sliding off with a bit of work. She tossed it on the desk and grinned. "Me."

Macy wanted to scream. To lunge at her. To run. "All this time, it was you?"

The look-alike stood before her and narrowed her brown eyes at Macy. "All. This. Time." She repeated. "It was so easy to be you, Macy. All I needed to get started was the spare key Uncle Robbie gave me because I'm such a dingbat and locked myself out." She smiled. "Then I placed some hidden cameras around the house so I could monitor your every move, duplicated your clothes, which I have to say would have been way harder had you had any fashion sense, and then set my plan in motion."

Sarah's head tilted as if she heard something and she put her finger to her lips. "Stay quiet. Someone's coming. Don't say a word if you want to learn the truth."

Macy clamped her lips together, doing her best not to make a sound.

A shadow passed under the door, then the knob rattled. "Anyone in there?" The voice of the young security guard asked.

Sarah shook her head and mouthed, "Don't."

Macy again fought back the instinct to cry out for help. She had to know what was happening and why.

The guard stood there another minute and tried the knob again, then walked away. They both listened intently as his footsteps disappeared down the hall.

Macy turned to face her fully. "Sarah, why?" Tears threatened to choke her. She didn't understand. "What have I ever done to you?"

"I'm not Sarah." She ground out through gritted teeth. "My name is Jodie. Does my name seem familiar to you?"

Macy muddled through her memories, the name faint, but not meaningful. "No, I'm sorry. I can't say it does."

"Well, that would be because you only knew me for the first couple years of your life." She ran her fingers through her long dark hair. "It seems funny that you can live with someone your entire life and never know them."

"What?" Macy couldn't believe her ears.

"Yeah, I had my own special room in our house. It was in the basement, specially decorated and furnished just for little… old… me." She laughed, but there was only malice in her expression.

Macy gasped. "That was you in the photos? You lived in that room?"

Jodie nodded. "Oh yes. You came to see me once. Do you remember?"

Macy's memory of the moment came rushing back. The chair she'd scooted to the door to see out. She wasn't trying to see out. She was trying to see in. Macy saw Jodie on the bed, shackled. Jodie looked up at her and grinned. Then her father caught her. He yelled at her for coming down there, her uncle ushered her up the stairs and told her mother what she'd done. She remembered asking her mother about the girl and her mother replying, "What girl? There's no girl. You're imagining things."

Jodie tilted her head. "I see it's coming back to you."

Macy's face bore the shock she felt. "Why were you down there?"

"Daddy dearest didn't think it was safe for me to live with the family anymore. I don't know where he got that idea. I didn't do anything too awful." She spoke each sentence with a dramatic flair.

Macy couldn't help her curiosity. "What *did* you do?"

Jodie shrugged. "I was five when you were born. I've

always been fascinated by how things work. So I loved to take things apart. I couldn't always put them back together though." Jodie looked Macy in the eyes. "Some things just don't go back together once we've dismantled them." She walked around the front of the desk and leaned against it. "My toys never lasted long. I wanted to see what made them tick, so to speak."

Macy felt the bile rise in her throat. Intuition told her she should leave, but she had to know why Jodie had been torturing her.

Jodie shrugged. "It was just innocent curiosity. But, the doctors felt different. They said it was a lack of empathy. That I had psychopathic tendencies." She sighed dramatically. "The priests said the devil possessed me. But the various exorcisms over the years were never effective. And the beatings… Well… let's just say daddy dearest and his friends thought they could beat the evil right out of me."

"Oh God." Macy frowned. "I'm so sorry. How could I have not known?"

Jodie slowly made her way around the room, eventually stopping and leaning against the door. "Oh, our entire household made sure I was a well-kept secret. Dad couldn't have the McCall name tarnished in anyway, so sending me to a mental hospital was out of the question. Instead, he set up his own little ward in our basement; soundproof rooms, shackles, drugs, electric shock… I had it all, little sister."

"But…" Macy was struggling to piece it all together. "They locked you up for tearing up a few toys?" Those weren't the parents she knew.

Jodie threw her head back and laughed. "No, they locked me up because when you were two I tried to suffocate you in your sleep."

Macy looked around the room in panic, her only exit

blocked. She remembered the journals she'd read. She'd thought he was speaking of her when her father mentioned his daughter, but he'd been talking about Jodie.

"I was sadly unsuccessful, as here you are. As for the toys, they didn't care so much about that. It was when I experimented on living things that they became upset. Ever wonder why you were never allowed pets, Macy?" She rolled her eyes. "They said I couldn't be trusted with animals or even insects."

Macy remembered once asking for a puppy and her mother almost hyperventilated as she tried to explain why it was impossible. Her parents had a different reasoning for the denial of every pet she'd requested.

"They weren't wrong. But what they did to me was unthinkable." Jodie's voice raised in volume and octave. "How could parents do that to their own child!" She huffed. "When you were born, they barely let me see you. I had to be supervised to spend any time with you at all. And they stopped spending time with me. Everything was about you after that. The child they prayed was normal. It's why you had to go, Macy. I didn't want you there."

"I didn't choose to be born, Jodie. You couldn't blame me for existing." Macy worked to keep the panic out of her voice. The person in front of her terrified her, more so now than when she thought she was simply a hallucination. The story she told she told went against everything Macy had ever believed about her family, and yet she knew it to be true. She had the faint memories, the photos, and the journals. Not to mention she saw the horrifying truth of the room herself.

"Oh, but I can blame you. You were the final nail in my coffin, metaphorically speaking. They wanted to keep you safe from me. They faked my death, saying I'd drowned in the pool. One of their doctor friends signed the death certificate to make it all official. Then they locked me away to begin treatments." She picked up a pen and twirled it between her fingers. "It's true, you know. Money can buy you anything."

"Jodie, none of that was right. None of it. There were and still are places where you can get proper help. They should have tried to help you and I'm sorry... so very, very sorry they didn't." Tears ran down Macy's cheeks as she thought of all her sister must have endured.

"I don't want help, Macy. I'm fine the way I am. But you. You poor, poor thing. You just couldn't live this way anymore. The loss from the fire-."

Macy interrupted. "Wait. How did you get out of the house if they chained you up in the basement?" Macy's mind raced to the painting for Mrs. Chase. The girl in the basement. Her memories of that scene flashing in her head once more.

"Dr. Britton came down to see me that night. He'd been especially cruel to me in recent days. And I didn't like the way he'd been looking at me. So, I flirted a little. He flirted back. And when his guard was down, I used my restraints to strangle him. Daddy came down to find out why he hadn't come back up. I ambushed him, knocked him out cold, and got the keys." Jodie had a look of pride on her face, as if she expected to impress Macy with her genius. "I dragged Dr. Britton into the secret room and set him in the chair. It wasn't easy, even with him being a small man, but I managed. I stabbed him a few times, for good measure, then tossed my bedsheet over his body. I'd unlocked myself with the plans to just get away. But as I was running through the foyer, I saw all the candles. Mother loved her candles. I picked one up and set it under a set of drapes in the living room. Then I did the same to the window setting in the foyer by the door. After that, it was simple to run through the lower level as I made my escape. Fires here, fires there. Fires everywhere." She chuckled. "I got out the back door just in time to see the entire lower level lit up. It was beautiful."

"Beautiful?" Macy shrieked. Her fear morphed into a rage. "You are insane. That fire killed everyone but me. It was horrific and painful and the reason I can barely function as an adult."

Jodie looked bored. "Don't be so dramatic. They all deserved it."

"Even Brandy? Miss Christy's daughter?" Macy shook her head. "No, there were innocent people in that house and you murdered them."

"No one in that house was innocent. They either took part, knew of me, or were guilty by association." Jodie spat as she moved closer to Macy.

"You killed Uncle Robbie." Macy wasn't revealing a big secret at that point, but she had to say it out loud. She needed to hear Jodie confirm it.

"He knew daddy had kept me locked away. He was as guilty as everyone else. And since you survived, and he didn't live with us, I had to make him pay too. Why not kill two birds with one stone? He dies and you go to jail for murdering him. I forgot to check your alibi for that night. Fucking Troy. I didn't expect him to drink the tea too."

"The tea." Macy whispered.

"Yeah, I'm kinda disappointed that you didn't put that together sooner. You are my sister, after all. I'd expected you to be smarter." She pretended to drink a cup of tea. "You're so predictable, Macy. A hot cup of tea was routine. All I had to do was swap out your regular tea for my special doctored tea when I needed you to pass out."

"You drugged my tea?" Macy struggled to believe her

ears, yet she also felt relief that she hadn't actually been blacking out.

"I did." Jodie smiled. "It's some combo of a date-rape drug and something else." She shrugged. "I dunno. It might have killed you, but we lucked out, didn't we?" She shook her head. "But Troy. He was a wild card I hadn't expected. I mean… I like the guy. And he's damn good in bed, but he's not really a keeper. I did you a favor by breaking up with him."

Macy couldn't stop the tears from falling. "I hate you."

She laughed. "I know. I'm such a mean older sister. That's how it's supposed to go, right? The older sibling picking on the younger sibling. But no worries. You won't have to hate me for long."

"Wh-what do you mean?" She still blocked Macy from getting to the door.

"Oh, that text you got from Dr. Yates? That was of course me, but no one knows that. You came here and broke in. He stood you up, and the rejection was more than you could handle. You killed yourself, right here in his office, with this gun." She pulled a revolver from her pocket. "It's Uncle Robbie's. Poetic, no?"

"You're sick." Macy stared at her. "No one will believe this."

"Sure they will." She moved to the desk, snatching up the paper from earlier and handing it to Macy.

Macy glanced at it, and her eyes flew to Jodie's.

"Read it. Out loud." Jodie smiled.

Macy had to clear her throat before she could start.

MY DEAREST DANIEL,

    I'VE TRIED TO DENY THIS THING BETWEEN

US FOR TOO LONG. I KNOW IT'S UNETHICAL FOR A PATIENT TO BE INVOLVED WITH HER DOCTOR, BUT WE WERE MEANT TO BE TOGETHER. I KNEW IT THE MOMENT I WALKED INTO YOUR OFFICE THE FIRST TIME.

I BELIEVED YOU FELT IT AS WELL, BUT DESPITE MY ATTEMPTS TO TELL YOU, YOU CONTINUE TO REJECT MY LOVE. I CAN NO LONGER LIVE WITH SO MUCH TRAUMA AND LOSS. YOU WERE THE LAST PIECE OF THIS TRAGIC PUZZLE I CALL A LIFE.

NO ONE WANTS ME AND ALL I HAD BEFORE MEETING YOU IS NOW GONE. IT'S TIME I END MY SUFFERING ONCE AND FOR ALL.

ETERNALLY YOURS,
MACY

She looked up from the letter and shook her head. "No one will believe I wrote this."

Jodie had the gun pointed at her. "They will. I've studied your journals. I know how you phrase your sentences and what words you would and wouldn't use. It sounds just like you."

Macy closed her eyes. Jodie was right, but she would not give her the satisfaction of letting her know she'd won. Not yet. Macy was going to go down fighting. She decided in that moment, that if she died, she was taking Jodie with her.

19

DANIEL

Daniel woke up and rolled over, his arm reaching for Sarah to pull her in close. The bed was empty and the spot where she'd slept was cold. He sat up and rubbed his face.

"Sarah?" He waited for an answer.

None came.

He got out of bed and limped to the bathroom, his leg stiff. He relieved himself, then washed his hands and face.

"Sarah? You still here?" He called once more.

Again, no answer.

He slipped back into his bedroom and pulled on his jeans. His cane leaned against the wall near the door, so he grabbed it on his way to the kitchen, leaning heavily on it as he moved.

Daniel looked around for any sign of Sarah. It wasn't like her to sneak out this way. She'd usually say goodbye, at least.

His phone dinged and caught his attention. *Why was it in the kitchen?* He usually kept it near his bed in case of a patient emergency.

He glanced at the time. It was only 11:00 p.m. He rarely

passed out so quickly or so early. The impromptu visit from Sarah was surprising, but the workout she'd gave him was very much welcome.

They'd made love before, but this time was urgent, needy, and a little rough, if he were honest. It was hot, but not his normal style. Sarah seemed to bring him new experiences with each encounter. The tea Sarah had fixed him after they'd had sex was delicious, and it wasn't his usual night-time drink, but she'd said it'd be better for him than whisky. She was trying to take care of him, and she was probably right. It seemed to relax him.

His phone pinged again, and he looked at the messages. Roger had sent him four messages, all with the urgent "call me now" in capital letters.

Alarm set him instantly on edge. He dialed Roger's number.

"Danny, dammit man, you are hard to get ahold of!" Roger bit out.

"Sorry, sorry. I was asleep and forgot to bring my phone into the bedroom. Is everything okay?"

"Well, not really." Roger sounded winded.

"What happened?" Daniel leaned against the counter, taking some weight off his bad leg.

"I saw your girl pass the bar window, so I ran out to say hello. She gave me a dirty look and kept walking."

Daniel frowned. "When was this?"

"About forty-five minutes ago." Roger said.

"And this was your emergency?" Daniel didn't know why Sarah was in that area after leaving his apartment, but he wasn't her keeper. She had a right to go where she wanted.

"No, my emergency is that I followed her for a while. She was acting suspicious to me. I saw her go into your office building. I knew you weren't there, and that set off some warning bells."

"You sent me a message because she went to my office?" Daniel thought it was odd as well, but maybe she knew someone else in the building? Even as he thought it, he knew that didn't seem right. She was new in town. She had no family and very few friends, if what she'd told him was the truth. If she'd known someone in his building, she'd have said something.

"Roger, thanks for the heads up. I'll call you back soon." He hung up without letting his best friend reply. Daniel had this slight nagging feeling ricocheting in the back of his mind for a while now, but he'd ignored it because he liked Sarah. He assumed it was his own paranoia barging in and trying to ruin a good thing. Right now, that feeling was as loud as a siren and telling him something was very wrong.

He closed his messages from Roger only to notice a message to Macy. One he hadn't sent.

MACY, MEET ME AT MY OFFICE AROUND 10:30. WE NEED TO DISCUSS WHAT HAPPENED.

What happened? He wasn't sure what that meant. *And who sent this to her from his phone?*

Sarah's face flashed in his mind. She had to have done it, but why? *Get to your office now* screamed through his mind as he rushed to get dressed. He hurried out of his apartment, forgetting his cane in his haste. Daniel would not let his leg slow him down this time, cane or not. He moved as quickly as his leg would allow, all but jumping in front of a cab to get it to stop.

"Where to?" The driver asked.

Daniel gave him the address and then shuffled through his text messages, assuring she'd sent Macy nothing else. He replayed all his conversations with Sarah. Everything he knew about her rolled together in his thoughts. How did she connect to Macy?

Nothing matched up. What was he missing? He wasn't sure, and that frustrated him.

He tossed cash at the cabbie as they pulled to a stop. "Thanks. Keep the change." He hopped out, and all but ran to the double doors of the building.

A younger guard, new to the job, met him in the lobby. "Dr. Yates. So glad you're here. Something odd is going on. A young woman-."

Daniel kept walking as briskly as he could, glancing at the guy's name tag. "Frank, is there a young woman in my office?" He answered.

"Uh, well. I don't know." Frank seemed puzzled. "I didn't realize you weren't here until after she'd made it up in the elevator. She said she was meeting you. She hasn't come down yet, but I went up to check and your office is locked up tight."

Daniel pushed the button, impatiently waiting for the doors to open. "C'mon!" He shouted. He turned to the older guard sitting behind the desk. "Was she alone? The young woman?"

"I believe so. I didn't see anyone else." The experienced guard replied.

Frank scratched his cheek. "I'm so sorry, sir. I'm new and I know sometimes you work late into the night. It didn't occur to me you might not be there."

"It's okay." Daniel replied. "I do often work late." He glanced at his watch. Not usually this late, but the kid felt bad already. He would not add to it at the moment. He had bigger worries.

The doors opened, and he rushed in, again pushing the button to the third floor and willing the thing to move.

Once it landed on the third floor, Daniel moved as quickly as he could down the hall but did his best not to make a sound. His tennis shoes were soft soled and made little noise if he were careful. He slowed even more as he neared his door. He thought he heard voices from inside. Daniel crept up to the door and tried to listen. He needed to understand what he was walking in on.

"No one will believe I wrote this." He heard Macy say.

"They will. I've studied your journals. I know how you phrase your sentences and what words you would and wouldn't use. It sounds just like you."

He was sure that was Sarah. What in the hell was happening in there?

"Jodie. No!" Macy shouted. "Let's work this out!"

Jodie? Who's Jodie?

"You have to die!" He heard the other voice reply.

He had to step in. He turned the knob, but it didn't budge. Daniel dug out his keys and quickly pushed it open.

Someone who looked exactly like Macy was holding Macy's arm, a gun pressed against her temple. The only reason he could tell the difference between the two was that one looked slightly older, and she was still wearing the clothes Sarah was had on earlier. His eyes shifted to the desk, and he saw the blonde wig.

"Hello, darling." Jodie murmured. "Why don't you come in and shut the door."

She pushed the gun into Macy's skin and he saw Macy wince. Without another thought, he did as directed.

Jodie nodded to a chair. "Take a seat."

He obeyed, keeping his eyes on them both. "You okay, Macy?"

She nodded ever so slightly.

Jodie pouted. "You care more about her than you do me? Typical. What is it with the men in my life? They all fawn over precious Macy. I'm the one that gave you amazing sex. I'm the one that was helping you get over that idiot Vanessa."

"Your name is Jodie?" He asked.

She smirked at him. "You sneak. You were listening at the door, were you? How much did you hear?"

He shook his head slowly. "Not much."

She shrugged. "You weren't supposed to be awake yet. I must have misjudged how much of the tea it'd take to knock out a man your size. Oh well. It doesn't matter. Looks like I'll have to change my plans," she glanced at the note in Macy's hand. "And that note."

Daniel worked to keep her preoccupied while he figured out the next course of action. "What do you mean?"

"Well, she was going to die of a self-inflicted gun-shot wound. But there's no reason the cops won't buy that she shot you, then herself. Murder-suicide. It's so romantic, don't you think?" Her voice held a mocking tone, and he grit his teeth, fighting back the urge to call her something nasty. He'd told her that in confidence and she was throwing it in his face.

"You're a bitch." Macy spat out.

Jodie grabbed her hair, yanking Macy's head back. "Shut. Up. Little sister."

Little sister? At least the resemblance now made sense.

"You don't have to do it this way, Jodie. We could let Macy go and you and I could go away somewhere. Paris? The Islands? Where would you like to go? I'll take you anywhere." He was throwing darts and hoping something would stick.

She gave him a mocking smile. "Aw, how sweet, Doc." She looked at Macy, then back at him. "But you're so wrong. She has to die. And so do you. Do you really think you meant anything to me? You were a means to an end, and now I'm done with you both."

Jodie was cold and indifferent now, not the woman he'd spent the last few weeks with. She could have taken to the stage with those acting skills. She'd fooled even him, someone trained to look for classic psychopathic traits.

"Do you really think people will buy this story of yours?" He needed to plant doubt in her mind. She had to believe she needed an alternative plan.

"I don't see why not." She replied. "I make a minor addition to the note. I shoot you, then help Macy shoot herself. Seems simple enough."

"Except you have to get out of here afterwards. The guard will see you." They must have both somehow missed seeing the blonde enter, but surely they wouldn't make that mistake twice. Especially after hearing gunshots.

"Oh, I've already got that planned out." Her smile made him uneasy. She opened her mouth to speak again, but this time the door flew open and interrupted her.

Roger stood on the other side, but he saw the gun a moment too late. Jodie fired and struck him. He fell out of sight and Macy screamed.

Jodie growled in frustration. "Fuck. Now I'll have to do this quickly before the guards get up here." She pointed the gun at Daniel.

Macy took a deep breath, then sank to the floor.

"God, your weak. Wake up, you little bitch." She shook Macy's arm, barely keeping her upright. As she bent over her, Macy elbowed Jodie in the face, causing blood to spurt from her nose.

She growled again as she lunged for Macy.

Macy rolled out of reach as Daniel tackled Jodie. He got a grip on the gun, but struggled to wrestle it from her hand. She tried to knee him between the legs, but he blocked most of the blow. Jodie slipped out from under him, and without hesitation, used the heel of her foot on his bad knee, smashing it with all her strength.

Daniel let out a howl of pain, the agony ripping through him in waves.

He glanced up through tears to see a glint of satisfaction on Jodie's face. Her hesitation to enjoy her work was all Macy needed to take her out at the knees and bring her down.

Daniel pivoted himself, trying to find ways he could be useful despite his now serious injury.

He heard footsteps running down the hall and knew that the security guards would join them at any moment. But it still might be too late. Roger was likely bleeding in the hall. He'd been crippled. And if Jodie got the better of Macy, they were all dead.

He focused on Macy and Jodie. Macy had climbed on Jodie's back and was pulling her hair violently. "Give me the fucking gun, Jodie!" She shouted.

Jodie tried to twist underneath her sister, the gun still firmly in her grip.

Daniel scooted closer to them, then kicked Jodie in the face, further breaking her nose.

The gun fell from her hands as she reached for her face. Macy grabbed it and hopped up. "Get your ass up." She shouted at Jodie as she pointed the gun in her direction.

Blood ran between Jodie's fingers as she covered the lower half of her face. She stood and glared at Macy, slowly placing herself between Macy and the door.

"You are going to spend the rest of your life in jail, Jodie McCall. I'll make sure of it."

Jodie shook her head. "I won't be a prisoner again. I'd rather die first."

In a quick move, Jodie reached for Macy, her bloody hands grasping at Macy's shirt.

Macy fired.

Jodie stopped moving, her eyes glancing down to her stomach, the blood spreading in a pool over her white shirt. She looked at Macy one last time, then stumbled backward, landing partially behind a large sofa that sat between them and the door.

Macy knelt next to Daniel. "Are you okay?"

He nodded. "I will be. Gonna need an ambulance or two, though. I think she hit Roger."

Macy stood and stepped toward the door. Daniel heard, "Freeze! Drop the gun!"

He saw Macy disappear, then stand back up. "It's not her! It's the other one!" He yelled through the door.

The older guard entered cautiously, noting Daniel on the floor. "Do you need help, Dr. Yates?"

"I do, but first make sure that woman is secured." Or dead, he thought hopefully.

"What woman?" The guard replied.

He pointed as he struggled to sit up. "The woman…" he stopped. Where Jodie had been previously was now a puddle of blood and smears. He could no longer see her, despite his vantage point from the floor on the other side of the room.

"Shit. Don't tell me she got away." He fell back against the carpet.

Macy stepped forward and leaned over the sofa. Alarm clear in her voice. "Where the hell did she go?"

The guard eyed them both oddly. "Did you both see her?"

Macy released a humorless laugh. Daniel could guess why. She'd been asking others that question for weeks.

Daniel looked at Macy. "I don't know where she went." His expression was grim.

"She's dangerous." Macy replied. "We have to find her."

Daniel nodded. "I agree. We'll have the police look for her." He tried to sit up straighter, but the pain from moving was almost unbearable. "Is Roger okay?"

She leaned into the hall and nodded. "He's just coming to. It looks like it didn't hit anything important."

"The hell it didn't." Roger yelled from the hallway. "I need my arm."

Daniel chuckled, relieved his friend was alright. "You passed out?"

He heard Roger moan again.

Macy sat next to him, waiting for the ambulance. "I'm sorry she pulled you into this."

He shook his head. "You are not at fault. It sounds like there are some deep-seated family issues there and she was at the center of them."

Macy shook her head. "I have an older sister I never knew about."

He attempted a smile, but the pain kept it subdued. "Hey, the plus side is you weren't hallucinating, and you don't have dissociative disorder."

She nodded. "Yes. True. I kind of wish I had been though." She sighed. "It's way less scary than knowing Jodie is out there, injured, and probably angry that her plans fell through."

"We'll make sure you're protected, now that we know what to protect you from." He looked heavenward. "Oh, thank God. The EMTs are here."

Macy stepped aside as they administered medical aide to

both Roger and Daniel. Oddly enough, she'd come out unscathed, physically. Mentally, he worried her paranoia would be worse until they found Jodie and locked her up. He could see the concern on her features every time she looked at the bloody mess where Jodie's body had lain.

Daniel listened as the police took her statement and inspected the evidence left behind. Daniel and Roger backed up her story about a dangerous look-alike on the loose.

He didn't know how Jodie had gotten out of the office without them seeing her, but she'd mentioned she had it all worked out before.

Macy followed as they loaded him into the ambulance. "Do you want me to come with you?"

He appreciated the effort it took for her to offer. "How about you call Troy and the both of you meet me at the hospital? We have some explaining to do and he needs to understand exactly what's been happening."

She nodded.

The ride to the hospital was rough, but they did their best to keep him comfortable. Jodie had broken his already badly damaged knee. Thankfully, he didn't need surgery, but he was going to be laid up for a while. He closed his eyes. That was fine. He really needed a vacation.

20

EVERYONE

roy pulled up in front of Dr. Yates' office. It relieved her he'd taken her call, especially after what happened the last time they spoke.

He jumped out, alarm in his voice. "Oh shit, are you okay?" He looked her over, looking for the injury that created the bloodstains on her clothes.

"I'm fine. It's not my blood." She gave him a weak grin.

"It's not." He repeated.

She nodded. "Can you take me to the hospital, I need to talk with Dr. Yates. He didn't come out of this so well."

Troy nodded. "You'll explain on the way?"

"Absolutely." She turned to watch an officer handcuff Frank, the young security guard. She shook her head.

He saw her and lunged, the officer yanking him backwards. "Hey lady. I'm so sorry. I didn't know what she was planning to do! She didn't tell me she was going to kill anyone! I swear!"

"Yeah, save it for your lawyer, pal." The officer said as he dragged him away and into a waiting police cruiser.

She clung to Troy. "I'm so sorry, Troy. I wouldn't blame you if you wanted to avoid me completely, but I hope you'll reconsider after I explain everything."

He ran a thumb over her cheek, wiping away blood and dirt. "I'll listen to whatever you have to say."

She smiled as he led her to his car.

It'd had been a month since Jodie disappeared. Despite a local manhunt, she seemed to have evaporated into thin air. Dr. Yates believed she went somewhere to hide and died there, sure that at some point someone would find her body and put the matter to rest. He was certain she couldn't have survived the gunshot without medical attention, and there had been no reports of her seeking help. Even with medical intervention, he felt sure she'd lost a lot of blood. She may not have survived, no matter who stepped in to help. Her guard boyfriend didn't have the training for such an undertaking, and they had arrested him shortly after helping her disappear. She never told him where she was going. She'd promised to contact Frank after things had cooled down, but as Macy suspected, that would not happen. He meant nothing to Jodie. No one did. He was another pawn in her game.

Macy tried to believe Jodie wouldn't be back, but deep down she wasn't so sure. Jodie had shaken Macy's life up too many times with her machinations. And while she now had a sad new viewpoint of her family, she still couldn't excuse the things Jodie had done.

Uncle Robbie had, like her father, left her his estate. Now that they had absolved her of any wrongdoing, she was clear to get the inheritance.

Troy proposed early, saying he couldn't wait for Christmas. And she was more than fine with that. She was tired of being alone.

She sold her home and the property, after allowing the police to clean up the disaster in the basement at her old house. Then she and Troy bought a small place in the suburbs where they sat outside in the breezy summer evenings and enjoyed the stars. They discussed wedding plans, possible pets, and even eventually, children.

Despite how it all started, Macy was happier than she'd ever been in her entire life. She still struggled with her anxieties and PTSD, but with the help of Troy and Dr. Yates, she was making remarkable progress.

The ocean waves crashed outside an open window. Dr. Raphael Fabrice inhaled the fresh salt air as he prepared for his next patient. He'd already had a full day, but this last-minute addition shouldn't take long.

A lovely young woman in a revealing dress entered and shook his hand.

He smiled at her and settled in before beginning his initial interview.

She returned his smile, her ruby red lips framing perfect white teeth. "Thank you for seeing me on such short notice, Dr. Fabrice."

He waved off her appreciation, noting her American accent. The tourists that came to Corsica had always fascinated him. They usually had such interesting stories to tell. He felt confident she had quite a story of her own. "It is nothing. How may I help you today?"

"Well," she twirled her long brown hair between her fingers. "I need to talk about my little sister."

He smiled. "I can certainly help you with that."

ACKNOWLEDGMENTS

Thank you for taking a chance on my first psychological thriller! This book was a work of passion and the product of an idea I'd been working on for years.

First and foremost, I owe a huge thanks to my husband, John. Without him most of these ideas I have would have died a horrid, lonely death in a drawer somewhere. He's the one who has supported me and been my side when I rejoiced about something exciting and when I cried about something disappointing. He's pushed me to keep going when I wasn't sure I could. He's my rock, the love of my life, and the reason I'm able to do what I do.

I owe another thanks to my BETA and ARC readers. They have helped me shape and mold this story into its final form. Huge hugs and kisses to Valerie Cooper, Kelly McCurdy, Brandi Cockrum, Anne Loshuk, Kristen Castellanos, Ashley Longcrier, Jeanette Reames, Hannah James, Kayla McDonald, Brandi Hecklelsmiller, Kat Bollinger, & Felicia Thorn.

I would be lost without my amazing editor Cheree Castellanos of For Love of Books4 Editing. She cleaned up the messy bits, filed down the rough edges, and helped me make sense of my scattered thoughts. Love you lady!

This badass cover was designed by the one and only Regina Wamba. If you need a cover that will blow your socks off, she's the lady to talk to. Thanks so much, Regina!

Thank you, dearest readers, for believing in me and my work. Sending you virtual hugs for all your love and support!

Since childhood, best-selling and award-winning author Amy Hale has been using the written word to inspire, encourage, and entertain. She loves creating characters and worlds from nothing but her imagination and a few glasses of wine. Her popular paranormal series, The Shadows Trilogy has earned multiple awards, as have the Havenwood Falls books, of which she is a participating author. She's also a participating author in the Feisty Heroines anthology which became a #1 New Release and Bestseller on Amazon, Barnes & Noble, and Nook shortly after its release.

She debuted her first fiction novel in 2015 after retiring from 13 years of non-fiction writing for various online entities. For the last couple of decades, she's also carried the titles of Laundry Goddess, Chef, Butt Wiper, Soother of Temper Tantrums, and in more recent years, Moderator of Sarcastic Eye-rolls and Sass. She resides in Illinois with her husband, a evil-genius dog, some reptiles, and around 20ish chickens.

If she had any spare time, she'd love music, photography, watching Mystery Science Theater 3000 with her family, and long rides on the back of her husband's motorcycle.

Learn more at http://www.authoramyhale.com

And subscribe to her newsletter at http://www.authoramyhale.com/newsletter

twitter.com/authoramyhale

instagram.com/authoramyhale